Beyond
A Tale of Discovery on the Other Side of Life

by
Ruth Mitchell

Ruth Mitchell

Publisher's Cataloging-in-Publication Data
Mitchell, Ruth
Beyond: A Tale of Discovery on the Other Side of Life
274 p., 20 cm.
ISBN: 978-0-578-81818-4

Cover design by Lorna Trigg / Wicker and Walker

Printed in the United States of America

Acknowledgements

This may sound a bit weird, but first on my list to thank are the characters in this book, including Cloud, Laura, Sean, Liam, Emily, Vincent, and even Dusty, a minor character, but he was actually the one who found Laura and saved her life. My adventure with these characters was so vivid I only hope I have presented them to you in this story in a way that you experience them with as much intensity as I have. Cloud, of course, is the hero of the story. I have used what is called an anthropomorphic literary device so that we may experience his viewpoint. No, he is not some silly talking dog, reminiscent of TV's Mr. Ed, but he represents the contribution to life that all God's creatures make.

Now to the people who have supported me during this time of creation and Covid. To my writing group: Chris Ritthaler, Charles Templeton, Selena Parrish, Danny Morris, and Wendy Taylor Carlisle. Virtual kisses and hugs all around for your varied and temperate sounding board. To the Writer's Colony of Dairy Hollow for providing a wider net of contacts than I might otherwise have. To Dan Krotz, an early reader, as well, to Lorna Trigg, the artist behind the beautiful cover, and most of all to Sarah Jennings of TechScribes Inc., whom I met accidentally – or was it a divine happenstance? – at a train meeting I went to with my husband, James Mitchell, who lives and breathes trains. Sarah has provided me with so much toward making this publication a success that words are inadequate.

Ruth Mitchell

'Two Moons of Meth'

"Computer, good morning."

Good morning. It's read a book day, so keep that in mind and enjoy a good book whether it's an old favorite or something new.

"Screw that! I'm trying to write a book, dammit!" As Laura pulls herself up off the sofa, the pain inside her skull erupts. "Oh Shit! You are just a dumb computer; you have no idea how my head aches."

According to the NIH: Different types of head-aches are treated differently. Migraine treatment is aimed at relieving symptoms and preventing additional attacks. Drug therapy, biofeedback training, stress reduction, and elimination of certain foods from the diet are the most common method of preventing and controlling migraine and other vascular headaches. Treating a tension-type headache involves...

"Stop! I only want to know what time it is. Always the smart ass. It's bourbon that caused this. What do you know, anyway? You are nothing but a stupid computer."

Hmm, I don't know that one.

Laura reaches around and grabs a small paperback from behind the sofa and throws it at her laptop on the desk. She misses, then panics because she might not have missed and could have knocked the flimsy, overpriced device off the desk. She keeps forgetting that every time she says the cue word "computer," the AI machine will make a comment.

She is behind schedule on the *Two Moons of Merth*, which she privately refers to by the nickname 'two moons of meth.' The pressure of finishing the book torments her every day. Even though she loves the characters in the story, she is struggling to pull it together. Her publishing company is already touting it as the next generation in her moderately successful series of fantasy novels.

The phone rings, and she frantically searches the crevices of the overstuffed couch for the *stupid thing*. When she finally puts her hands on it, it is only Dusty calling to see if she wants him to walk the dog for her today. She punches the "I can't talk right now" button and switches the correspondence to text.

...Don't worry about Cloud today I need to get some exercise myself. I spent all day yesterday and only wrote two pages. I need to clear my head...

...k...

Dusty texts back.

Cloud is Laura's imposing white Shepherd, curled up in the down cushions he has stomped into a nest beside her. They have spent the night there as Laura had gotten too smashed to move the party to the bedroom. Remnants of a popcorn microwave bag are scattered around on the floor where Cloud has polished off the last burnt kernels after she passed out. Now he is licking his chops, savoring the last lick of mint chocolate chip ice cream once puddled in the blue ceramic dish on the coffee table. Laura sometimes forgets to feed him once she hits the sauce, and so he must be resourceful.

She never forgets to finish off her bourbon, Cloud thinks. He had tried it once when one of her precious bottles had overturned leaving a pool on the floor with its richly disturbing aromatic fumes. *Despite its absurdly interesting taste, it left me feeling weird, like I only had three legs. Nope, don't need to try that stuff again.*

The "W" Word

"Would you like that baby?" Laura looks at him and caresses the beautiful white dog's head. "How about I take you for your walk today?"

The most critical issue for Cloud right now is he has heard Laura say the "W" word.

He looks at her plaintively and starts to gently whine. Their relationship is symbiotic of course, but Cloud, without any formal training, has slipped into the role of Laura's service dog. Now lest she forgets her promise, he jumps up, pulls his leash off the kitchen table, and rushes to the door where he barks, looking expectantly at Laura.

"Whoa kiddo," Laura stumbles up from the couch. "I've got to shower and get dressed." The silk kimono she uses as a bathrobe for lounging around her enormous penthouse is dangling off one shoulder like a piece of cellophane wrap infected with static. It clings persistently to her thighs.

Before stepping into the shower, Laura admires her body in the mirror wall that will soon be steamed up. She is addicted to the idea of staying thin. *Not bad. I still can't ease up and let the weight get out of hand. Remember when you thought it was okay to only eat dessert for dinner? Wait, I pretty much did that last night. Got to get more exercise, blah, blah, blah.* She annoys herself with her obsessions, and when this is not enough begins scolding herself for binging on bourbon last night. *If things would only come together on the new work.* Despite Laura's experience with five completed books, living the solitary life in front of a computer screen is not always ideal, even if she owns a moderately successful boutique hotel and could have room service for every meal.

I need some variety in my life. I'll make a pitcher of margaritas tonight. That's much more sociable than bourbon. She rubs the artisan-made soap across her wet belly. It is the same all-natural soap made locally, wrapped in rice paper, and placed in the ceramic soap dishes in each room in the Crescent. It makes her body smell like lavender laced with wildflowers.

While Laura takes her sweet time luxuriating in the shower, Cloud paces neurotically around the suite passing the four-poster bed with its intricately carved pedestals, through the sun-dappled living room, past the office where he and Laura spend so much time, with its wall to wall books, until he ends up in the recently updated kitchen with its parquet flooring, stately white cabinets, and mottled granite counters. None of this is important to him except the refrigerator, the storage bin where his food is kept, and most of all, the drawer with the big bag of addictively flavored treats, which Laura refers to as "puppy crack."

Finally, she shows up in her jogging attire, although based on last night's binge drinking, *there probably won't be too much of that going on.* Cloud can be Laura's worst critic.

Laura and Cloud finally make their way to the antique elevator with its collapsible brass scissor gate. Cloud sits patiently like a well-bred gentleman as the rickety elevator makes its way up, clicking and banging until it reaches the eighth floor of the notoriously haunted hotel Laura inherited from her eccentric grandmother.

Cloud leans down and sniffs the worn carpet in front of the elevator. *French fries!* The elevator chugs up one more floor with a noisy lurch and lands at their feet. *Great, no ghosts in the elevator.* Cloud has grown used to seeing the apparitions float in and out of rooms or take strolls down the hallways, but he's not too keen on riding in the elevator with them. *It's too close for comfort.*

The decrepit elevator makes the same noises as it lurches downward toward the lobby. It always takes some time to make their way through the rabbit hole that is the lobby. Laura has to stop and talk to employees, and tourists want to pet Cloud, *because I am so beautiful.* He resigns himself to the delay by pulling at the leash until she drops it. He chooses a warm spot next to the massive stone fireplace where logs crackle with energy and purpose beneath the dramatic and beautiful portrait of Laura's grandmother, from whom she inherited the hotel.

Laura gets into a lengthy conversation with Liam, the manager of the hotel who has spied Laura trying to sneak past him. Liam surely has some pressing issue to discuss, because Laura only meets with him once a week, and he inevitably has questions on a daily basis that must be answered. Liam is a perfectionist. He gets his edgy purpose from his background as a Swiss-trained hotelier.

Eventually, they make it outside. Cloud's nostrils flare in wild anticipation of all the many things he will learn on this walk, like who peed on the big granite rock or if there were any squirrels eating berries over by the fountain in the garden. And yet he does not pull at his leash like some dogs might. Cloud takes pride in his obedience to Laura. Besides, if there are only a few people in the park today Laura will unleash him and then *heaven!* Although he will not get out of her sight, because he *needs to keep tabs on her,* he will be free. *Glorious freedom is what I deserve with all the discipline I exhibit day in and day out.*

The sights and smells of Huntington Park are like Chopin to Cloud. His hearing is so keen he can recognize the difference between a lizard and a skink by the way they walk through the leaves. Several neutered dogs have already passed this way as well as one female who is not in heat. *Too bad.*

It's not until they have finished their walk and are returning that Cloud notices Laura looking at her phone more frequently than usual.

"Well, buddy" she looks down to re-hook the leash. "It looks like we have to go to New York." Her expression is unusually difficult for Cloud to read. *Wait, Cloud thinks, is this a good thing or a bad thing? She said we, so does that mean I get to go to New York? What is a New York anyway? Will they have bones there, and what will the food be like?"*

"My publisher wants to have a face to face. It's okay, he's going to pay for everything. So that means you can come too and stay in a fancy hotel. We'll book one close to Central Park and we can go for long walks there too, only you will have to wear your service halter on the plane. I know it's a sham, but those are the rules."

Cloud has no more time to ponder Laura's news because a squirrel has darted right in front of him like a hussy flirtatiously lifting her skirt. He sits obediently. His discipline, coupled with the look of desire he gives her, impresses Laura enough to respond sympathetically by letting him loose once more before they head back. He looks back at her gratefully as he darts off for a few moments of unbridled passion.

Stalled

"Computer what time is it?

It's 3:22 p.m.

Laura looks over at Cloud who is lying on the floor staring at the box lunch they picked up downstairs earlier, as if it might disappear were, he to let go of his steady gaze. Laura's stomach makes a growling noise.

To emphasize his hunger, Cloud whines a little and lets his eyes dart back from the box filled with a juicy roast beef sandwich to hers and once more back to the box in case she didn't get the cue.

"Okay, I get it." She springs up from the desk and takes the box over to the window seat where they can eat and stare out at the city below. Cloud loves the window seat for the same reasons Laura does, the view and the cacophony of bright pillows scattered across it. He nestles in to wait. Then she gets up again and goes to the kitchen to pour some lemonade.

This is good, no bourbon. If she starts with the bourbon this early in the day, it could get messy.

"So, I've thought a lot about taking you to New York, and I'm thinking it's going to be too much of a hassle. You'd be better off staying here and Dusty will come and take care of you."

Dusty, of course. That sounds better than a visit to New York. Not sure what a New York is anyway. Laura pinches off another meaty bite and says to him. "You've had your walk, you've had your lunch and now I've got to get back to work."

Laura's phone buzzes, signaling a text message.

...Going to dinner with me tonight? You promised...

Laura texts her friend Tessa back

...no gotta work...

...you need to get out and have some fun. There's a band at Buffy's tonight...

That's a little pushy. Still, she hadn't seen Tessa in a while. The last time she went out with her she had ended up in bed with a total stranger. A smile creeps across Laura's face. *Maybe that will happen this time.*

Getting back to her desk, Laura feels stalled. "Computer good afternoon"

Good afternoon. Today is Indigenous People's Day, Indian Day, or Native American Day, honoring diverse and enduring cultures from all over the world. Indigenous people, also known as Aboriginal peoples or Native peoples, are those who inhabited a country or geographical region at a time when people of different cultures or ethnic origins arrived. There are estimated to be more than 370 million Indigenous people throughout more than 90 countries worldwide. Many Indigenous people still maintain traditional cultural practices, such as their native languages, belief systems, social

structure, farming, and strong connection to their ancestral lands. In my home state of Washington, the Muckleshoot tribe has lived throughout the Green and White River watersheds, speaking their ancestral language, Luhootseed, for the last 10,000 years.

Wow, perfect, here I am writing about similar people on another planet. Laura's brain is on fire now. The neurons are volleying ideas playfully across her frontal lobe.

She is ready to get to work, although she's not trying to portray a specific Indigenous group or concerned where they are located. In fact, she is specifically keeping the backdrop of her new book pristinely clean like a blank canvas. Instead, she wants to take the reader into a cultural vacuum where she can focus purely on the thoughts of her heroine as she develops from a young innocent to a leader of thousands. The key element in Aayda's culture is that it has not been disturbed yet by a conquering culture.

Laura types:

The earth trembles as the buck comes driving toward me. His hooves pound deep into the soft earth. I dive out of his way or be trampled! Picking myself up off of the forest floor and brushing off the leaves I wonder, was that an apparition or perhaps an omen? Was it real?

"Computer how do you field dress a deer?"

Sorry I don't have the answer to that.

"Of course, you don't. Dammit." Laura Googles the topic so she can move on. Gruesome stuff, though her heroine Aadya, who had just felled a large buck, would need to know.

I'm not sure where this is going. I'm not sure I like it. Laura is as puzzled as if she was reading someone else's work. *Where was this coming from?* She pushes her chair away from the desk disgustedly and goes to the bar, a massive German sideboard that houses an excessive variety of bottles to fulfill any wanton appetite. She puts her hand on the bottle of bourbon front and center of the marble slab then hesitates. *I'm going out tonight and shouldn't drink in broad daylight.* So instead of pouring a glass she takes out one of the small joints she keeps in reserve for just such an occasion and pours a tall glass of lemonade. "Come on Cloud let's go sit out on the veranda. Cloud cocks his head at her and whines. "Come on for a little while, then I'll feed you. Don't be such a big baby."

I am not a big baby! I am a titan of discipline, for God's sake. Haven't you noticed?

Eventually Laura gets the munchies, and she goes and gets some cheese and crackers. Cloud's share fills him up for the time being.

The sun gets low in the sky and the flagstone veranda is no longer feeling cozy. Cloud barks at the French doors, insisting that Laura pay attention. Snacks are over, it's time for the meal. *Let's have some meat!*

Once inside, Cloud senses the presence of a ghost that has gone astray and is wandering into their suite. It's a child who is chasing a ball with a stick. *This is not al-*

lowed! Cloud gives a deep guttural growl, and his ruff goes up. Almost as if the ghost child understands, he looks up and stares wide-eyed at Cloud, turning and running toward the wall from which he had come. A trickle of sparkly lights like tiny fireflies follow in his wake.

A Night on the Town

This is so dumb, what am I doing here? Laura looks around the room of the dark and gloomy bar, where everyone seems so happy. That's the point of bars isn't it? A place where people come together to be cheery and socialize. She looks around the room. *There's not a single doable man here.*

Laura looks at Tessa, leans over and talks loudly into her ear. "I think the music upstairs sounds intriguing, why don't we go up there?" Tessa nods affirmatively and they gather their purses and climb the stairs. The atmosphere is totally different in the loft and Laura perks up.

"We'll have to order food if we stay here." Tessa warns her.

"I love this music!" For Laura it's a no brainer. A handsome man has an electrified cello between his legs and the music emanating from his instrument is sending tingling sensations into her tequila-soaked neurons. Her frontal lobe is alive with prickly lights and her limbic system is purring.

They sit at a small round table with a white linen cloth and order steaks. *Mmm, this is good. I could listen to this man all night. No, I could look at him all night.*

While the music is hypnotic it is a little loud and brilliant for dinner conversation. The waiter brings a velvety Pinot Noir, and so they settle in. They finish off their satisfying dinner with a tiny raspberry tart topped with a splotch of fresh whip cream. As the buttery tart sensation hits Laura's taste buds, the musician signs off for the night.

The next thing Laura knows is he is standing at their table.

"We enjoyed your performance," she says, about two wine glasses beyond the ability to feel self-conscious. This man she has been lusting after for the past hour is now close enough to touch.

"Won't you join us?" Tessa looks around and points to an empty chair.

"Why thank you ladies. You are most kind," he says as he pulls it up to their table. Tessa signals to their waiter that they'd like another bottle of wine and a third glass.

Tessa makes a damn good wingman. At the beginning of the evening Tessa, who was from Texas had said to her "What you need is a good romp in the hay."

"Oh, please, that expression is so corny." Laura had admonished her.

Now this gorgeous man has materialized in front of her and she is ready for whatever is next.

Generally, Laura does not bring men back to her place because she doesn't like the hotel staff gossiping about her. This had provided for a couple of interesting liaisons though tonight's hookup goes smoothly. Hartford Kensington had been reserved an adequate suite at the adjoining hotel as part of his compensation package. Turns out he is as good at sex as he is at playing the electrified cello.

The next morning Laura lets Harford order her sausage and scrambled eggs delivered to the room. They engage in mild conversational chatter about his career as a musician.

"What do you do?" he finally gets around to asking. It's a question she has fielded many times before and prefers to be mis-directional like a magician. Though she has written hundreds of thousands of words in her career, explaining what she does in a conversation is not something she enjoys. No one, unless they have authored a novel themselves can possibly understand the insanity of it. It was worse if she told them she owned a hotel.

Meanwhile, Cloud has spent a restless night intermittently dozing on the big plush couch, where he has an unobstructed view of the door, and pacing randomly around the suite waiting for Laura to come home. Every time the clock in the hall chimes, he wakes up and stirs around to no avail. He entertains the thought of going into the bathroom and knocking over the waste can, spilling its contents and spreading them across the room. He has resisted this recreant behavior until about 4 a.m. *That's it, she needs to be punished for her behavior. I'm not putting up with this shit!*

Finally, after the sun is well into the sky, Cloud hears the key turn in the door.

"Hey pookey!" Laura is cheerful and her clothes are crumpled. Cloud lets the big white flag of affection that is his tail, flap and wave. All is forgiven, as he catches a whiff of red meat.

"Did you miss me? Here I brought you something." She opens a mangled, white paper sack stained with blood, and drops the tidbits into his bowl. He barks with gratitude and inhales the meat. All is forgiven. Whatever indiscretion Laura had suffered upon him, is now null and void.

The Big Apple

Laura and Cloud have the "you're going to New York – you're not going to New York" conversation until Cloud becomes so *over not going to New York* that he purposely gets a stone bruise on his paw and limps around the suite until she finally concedes he shouldn't go to New York. *Damn the things I have to do around here to get my way*!

Laura curls up on the sofa with him and explains how much happier he will be if he stays home.

"Dusty will walk you every day. And feed you. I have a very full schedule. Maybe another time we can go so you can see Central Park, you and I, no agenda."

Laura had been to New York twice before, and like everyone else who ever touched the concrete shores of "The City that Never Sleeps," she is enthralled by the lights, the buildings the people thin and stern as they rush to their next appointment, charmingly oblivious to the spell their city casts on visitors.

"So, Stuart, where are you taking me to dinner?" She asks as she slips into the Town Car with her editor. Her sateen skirt slides her across the leather seats like a puck on ice. She has already had two martinis at the St. Regis bar where she is staying, across from Central Park.

Stuart pats her on the leg in a brotherly fashion and says, "Oh, honey, this night is just for you. I thought we would go to the 21 Club and do some celeb sightings."

"Really? You think we'll see some movie stars?" *The thought of running into Brad Pitt or George Clooney seemed immensely funny.*

"Seriously, am I dressed up enough? I had a difficult time deciding what to bring and then I had a hard time deciding what to wear tonight. I work in my pajamas a lot."

Instead of laughing at the intended joke, Stuart frowns. *What is the undercurrent going on here?*

Again, he pats her leg just above the knee on the shimmering pale green cloth of her skirt, more suitable for stroking, than for patting.

"Laura dear, I'm getting a little concerned for you."

"What? Stuart. What are you talking about? I'm making substantial progress on the book," she lies.

He looks at her seemingly biting his tongue, unsure of his next words.

Oh shit! Shouldn't have had that second martini.

"It's not only that Laura. To date you've been successful, but I've been in this business too long not to see what is happening to you." He grasps her hand and curls it inside of his in a mini hand embrace.

"Many writers, when they reach a certain level of … They, well, they get tangled up in booze and drugs. I see the tell-tale signs here."

"What the fuck are you talking about Stuart?" *Oops, too strong.*

"Laura you know I think the world of you, but I've had several alarming late-night phone calls from you.

What is he talking about? Best to bait and switch at this point. "I must be a quarter of the way through the book already. You needn't be concerned. I am holding up my end of the bargain."

Stuart looks down his glasses at her, and perhaps he decides this line of conversation isn't going anywhere either.

"Your deadline is May 30. That's a hard deadline, Laura, a hard and fast deadline."

Surprisingly at dinner Stuart orders a bottle of 2009 Dom Perignon for them to share, and with dinner, a Côte de Bordeaux Cabernet Sauvignon. *He's sucking that stuff down himself What's the deal?*

"I need you to agree to some interviews, Laura. Not this week, but we need to start lining some up. May will be here before you know it and we need to start promoting the new title. We can do these by phone. I will be conducting these interviews from my office. I will call you first, preferably in the morning see if things are, ah, suitable with you, and the interview will be somewhat supervised by me. That way we can insure a best-case outcome."

This whole evening has taken some bizarre twists, though it is good to see Stuart taking the promotion of my new book seriously. Maybe I do need to straighten up a little.

"Oh, and I have a little surprise for you tomorrow. I have arranged a meeting with a ghost specialist. He's a friend of a friend, and when I mentioned how one of my authors lived above one of the most famous haunted hotels in the country, this guy got in touch with me.

"He wants to interview you and do a personal story. I think this will do a world of good for raising your personae in the general public. Who knows, it may lead to a talk show."

The wheels buzz frantically in her head, while they have promoted the 1862 luxury hotel in this way, to the point of having greatly profitable ghost tours, the hotel is her home.

"I'm not sure, I'll need to check with my manager."

"Liam? Please, he'll be totally onboard for this opportunity. I'm telling you this is a great hook; I can't believe we haven't already mined this field." Stuart was practically vibrating now. *How can I possibly say no?*

"I'll have a car pick you up at 9:30. Be ready."

Laura's first glimpse of Sean Wilson is from the back when she enters Stuart's office, so she doesn't see his eyes until he stands to shake her hand. He reminds her of a young Pierce Brosnan, only with a more rugged demeanor. His startling magnetism makes her feel unlaced, like a floozy coming out of her bustier.

"How do you do?" she musters up as she sticks out her hand to shake his. *That sucked!*

If his disarming green eyes were not enough, what happens next almost knocks her over. "So, pleased to meet ya'. Stuart here has been fillin' me in on your situation. I love San Francisco and can't wait to come stay in your hotel and study it."

That accent, is it Scottish? It's not some sort of weird British dialect? Pinch me now, did he just say he was coming to the Crescent?

"I'm sorry, I thought I was here for an interview." She glanced over at Stuart for some visual cues.

"Forgive me," Sean is still holding onto her hand, clasping it now in less of a handshake, and more of a gentle grip as if he were offering condolences to an elderly aunt. "We've been havin' a conversation before you arrived."

"Let me bring you up to speed," Stuart offers. "Sean here is a world-renowned paranormal researcher, and while I thought it would be good to bring you together for an interview, he is much more interested in seeing for himself if your hotel is really haunted. I think this will make a much more interesting portrayal. In fact, it might well make a goddamn mini-series!"

"Stuart, slow down," she turns toward Sean. Not surprisingly she is still knocked off center when she looks at this man with the piercing green eyes. "What does this entail?"

"Well I would bring a team of four plus myself, and some equipment. We are at the forefront of this research with our use of Artificial Intelligence. I have actually already familiarized myself with your hotel, which once served as a home for unwed mothers after its heyday. Correct?

"But first you must be curious about my company," He rambles on not giving her a chance to answer his question. "We are now located in Connecticut, but I got my start in Scotland, as a kid, working for my aunt and uncle, Maria and Evan Robertson."

"He's very well respected," Stuart assures her.

Laura finally sits down in one of the two visitors chairs across from Stuart's desk. It swivels so she can point herself toward Wilson who follows her cue and sits down too.

"I'll have to run this past my manager. When are you thinking?"

"Well, soon. It will take a few days to assemble the players. We have a big project right now in Salem."

"Salem, Massachusetts?"

"Yeah," he smiles, "It's a little obvious, but we find more activity where there are pockets of cultural massing."

"Makes sense."

"Ours is not considered a science, because the general population is not psychic. So, few people are able to accept our findings because they can't experience it for themselves. We have been makin' great strides with our AI equipment though, which we will pair and use in conjunction with all our tools, includin' a paranormal seein' eye dog."

"What?"

Sean smiles, absolutely breaking her heart even if he is coming off as a bit self-promotional.

Sounds intriguing and would give the hotel even more notoriety, unless of course they debunk the hauntings. She keeps her concerns to herself.

"While I haven't discussed this with Stuart," Sean says as he looks in the direction of their host, Stuart, who sits behind his desk large enough to serve as an aircraft carrier for small airplane models. "There is always the possibility that our experiments will be picked up by one of the networks, or even FilmFlix. We film everything ourselves and post it on our website. One of our young recruits is related to a producer over at FilmFlix and we have been discussin' possibilities."

Laura looks toward Stuart, "I can't believe I am saying this, but this could BE a mini-series."

"Damn, don't you know it!" Stuart claps his hands together silently like a little kid.

"Hey baby I'm home!" Laura crashes through the door with her luggage.

Cloud leaps up and runs to her, completely forgetting his manners. He jumps up on her barking giddily. *God, I can't believe you are finally home. It's been deadly quiet here. I've been so lonely. You smell exotic, like many people and places I've never known before. This must be what a New York is.*

"Oh my, so much to tell you about buddy." She hugs him back. "First I've got to pee and then I want to take a long soak in the jacuzzi."

Preparing for Something

"Computer what time is it?

It's 1:32 a.m.

Oh my, I guess I need to get some sleep. Laura shuts her laptop and looks over at Cloud who is currently sprawled across the king-sized bed. He snores softly. She pats him gently on the hindquarters. He doesn't even raise his head, so she has to squeeze in and around him to get under the covers.

Since returning from New York, Laura has been working harder, avoiding booze and getting more exercise. It seems that Stuart has put the fire to her feet, and she is taking her commitment more seriously. *Or is it really that? No, definitely not. For the first time in a long time I'm looking forward to something! Sean Wilson will be here within the week. Thursday, next Thursday. I have a shitload of things to do before then. Mostly get this book off dead center.*

Laura looks around at the large bedroom. The gas fireplace still burns, with its cozy flickering. *Still can't sleep. It's either have a nightcap or keep writing.*

She heads to the bar a little chilled and jittery. *I worked hard all day; a shot of bourbon will help me sleep.* With her glass in hand she must work her way back into the bed. This time she manages to move Cloud over a bit. It doesn't take long for the bourbon to kick in and she eases into sleep like a cat curled in the sunshine. She starts dreaming of Liam of all people.

29

"Laura, I have to tell you the ghosts here are not real. You can't have these ghostbusters come and investigate because they will debunk our ghosts and a whole income stream of ours will be history. You must tell these people they can't come. It will disrupt the entire hotel and hurt us."

No, no, she is trying to tell Liam in her dream. Everything will be okay. I've felt their presence myself and Cloud sometimes barks at things when nothing is there. You mustn't be afraid Liam. We have to do this. I can feel it.

Waking up in her bed the sun is already high in the sky and the fog is gone. Laura calls room service to have coffee, granola and her smoothie sent up. She goes to feed Cloud and opens wide the double French doors to the veranda letting the warmth of the sun remind her she is alive as she stretches out the kinks. In the next room Cloud barks once, his 'come notice something is going on bark,' and she is relieved to see her over-sized latte has arrived and she can get back to work.

...Dusty you're on duty this morning...

...k...

He texts back.

Laura pulls on some sweats and pulls out the laptop. Cloud lays down by the door waiting for Dusty to come and Laura texts the hotel kitchen for more coffee.

"Computer what time is my hair appointment tomorrow?"

Your hair appointment is at 11:00 a.m. With a massage following at 1:45.

Damn, I wish I hadn't booked so much at lunch time. "Computer, order me a Reuben to be delivered to the Spa at 12:30 tomorrow."

Your order has been sent to the kitchen.

Except for last night's nightcap it has been three agonizing days without booze. Laura shuts her laptop and, like a compass drawn to true North, heads to the massive sideboard she inherited from her Grandmother to pour a small hit of bourbon. Seeing her get up, Cloud trots after her. He barks once to get her attention. She looks at him. "I guess you're right, we should go for a little run. Let's go hit the park first."

Damn right. You act like you've forgotten I exist. He decides they'd better take the ball throw. Cloud goes over to the closet where it is kept and barks once to focus her on the matters at hand. *Yay, Laura notices.* She reaches in and gets the ball and plastic chuckit, and then goes back over to the bar to throw the amber liquid down her throat.

They head out to Pioneer Park, one of Cloud's favorite places, and spend over an hour chasing the ball. Once he experiences a nice mellow glow from the exercise, Cloud signals he is ready to stop. *So many smells to ponder and not enough time.*

"Good boy," Laura tells him numerous times and strokes him casually on the head and neck. "After tomorrow things might get a little hectic, Cloud. A crew is coming in to study our ghosts." Cloud looks out across the bay at the shimmering expanse beneath him and does not judge. *It is clear from her peculiar behavior, the long hours of writing, the cutback on the drinking and her overall demeanor that Laura is preparing for something, but I don't know what it is.*

The next day Laura is gone a lot and Cloud notices she is a bit more edgy than usual. When she returns he senses a change. *Damn, she's looking good, almost mellow.* Later in the day he watches as she struggles with the idea of drinking and sadly as she gives into her desires. He makes sure she doesn't forget to feed him and then settles in for a quiet night of TV on the couch and snacks galore; snacks freely given and later when Laura passes out, snacks freely taken.

Everything Changes

Thursday comes and Cloud's life changes forever, with a simple knock on the door of their suite. He barks once and stares at the door in case Laura didn't hear. She is unusually responsive and leaps up from her desk to open it. There stands a man smelling of potato chips and barbecue sauce. Not only that, he has with him a beautiful black and white female border collie. *This is highly unusual, but what a sweet-smelling girl!*

"Sean, it's great to see you!" She says to the man dressed in jeans, a plaid shirt, and wearing a sports jacket made of leather the same color as his shoes. Cloud makes a quiet, but not too unfriendly, guttural noise to let everyone understand he is in charge.

"I told you I would be bringin' Daisy, right?" Laura looks down at Daisy and says, "All are welcome."

"It's fantastic. She has already signaled to me several times, from the lobby to here. If only she could talk, my job would be much easier."

You got that right sonny! When you people finally get your act together and learn our language, we'll all be better off. We've been listening to your drivel for centuries now. And you sir, have an especially annoying way of speaking English.

Cloud sniffs out Daisy who trots over to the window seat and boldly jumps up on Cloud's cushions. *Damn girl, you get right to it.*

"My crew is waiting for me downstairs, I just wanted to check in with yoo."

"Did they show you to your rooms and check you in?"

"Yeah, and I will be meetin' with your manager this afternoon to go over our work schedule. We also need to coordinate with your ghost-tour guy."

"Okay, keep me posted, they will be the people you need to coordinate with. I'll be here if you need me for anything." Sean whistles one quick burst and Daisy responds immediately, her tail wagging.

"Computer, text Sean and invite him up for dinner, no wait, tell him I will meet him at the Crystal Ball Room at 7 o'clock if that is convenient for him.

Done. Message sent.

"Computer what time is it now?"

4:30 p.m.

Laura pulls her legs down off the desk and shuts her laptop. She is stiff from being in the same position too long.

Cloud jumps off the couch and noses Laura determinedly. *If we don't go now, we'll run out of daylight. Besides, those apparitions have been oozing through the walls unexpectedly all day long like something was stirring them up. We should get out of here for a while.*

Laura touches the soft hair on the top of Cloud's head and lets her hand graze his pointed ears, squeezing them

34

as if to check if they are real. "You read my mind kiddo. Let's get outt'a here."

"So how did the first day go?" Laura asks Sean once they are seated at her favorite table with a view of the Bay. The Crystal Ballroom is a stunning Victorian assimilation of mirrors, glass, and of course crystal chandeliers. Hanging on the walls are heavily framed landscapes and other art Laura's grandmother collected during her lifetime.

"It's lookin' promising. We recorded a lot of activity, but our real work begins in the wee hours of the morning."

"Why is that?"

Sean shrugs, "I dunno' I suppose it has to do with stillness. When the world quiets down we can hear the spirits better."

"Bring us a bottle of MaCrostie Pinot Noir, please" Laura asks the waiter, thinking that if she sticks to wine, perhaps she won't get too toasted.

"Oh, no thanks, I don't drink," Sean tells her.

"Oh?" *Shit, I should have had another bourbon before I came down here.* Laura looks at the waiter who knows her tastes. All they need is eye contact to affirm that he will bring her the wine she asked for.

"Well, I hate to drink alone, but this meal will be fabulous, and the wine will only enhance Chef's choices. He is preparing us a special dinner. Are you sure you won't change your mind?"

Sean looks down for a minute then looks back up to her. I haven't had a drink in over 19 months."

"Oooh, I get it. Sorry I didn't mean to be pushy." *I hope Tod hurries up with that wine. I'm so fricking thirsty.*

Laura looks at Sean, hungry to ask him direct questions and not sure of her own judgment. She decides to jump right in. "Is this a dog and pony show or are there really ghosts?"

He flashes her that killer smile. "You don't waste much time gettin' to brass tacks, do yoo? Actually, science now days is becomin' our friend. Quantum physics research is openin' doors to the coexistence of other dimensions and realities." He takes a bite and launches into a dialogue he has obviously spoken many times before.

"Ghost, spirits, or whatever you want to call paranormal beings, have always been an integral part of most human cultures," he explains while unfolding his napkin with somewhat of a flourish. "Why some people are able to see these beings and others are not is hard to say, but our dog Daisy, who you met, can see them for shoor. She has a way of communicating with us through standard dog signals as to what she is seein.'"

"That must be like teaching the apes to communicate with us through sign language."

"That's a good analogy," Sean nods affirmatively.

"My standard spiel is this: You understand electricity and radio waves without being able to see them, right?" He sips on his water and meets her gaze. "There are over 15,000 radio stations in the U.S. alone and you can tune into those stations sometimes from opposite sides of the world. You can't perceive these energy transmissions without a radio, but tens of thousands of them coexist simultaneously. If you had talked about radio a hundred years before it became common, people would have thought you were a lunatic."

The waiter brings the wine and wants to make a flourish of serving it. "That's fine Tod I know it's good."

Sipping the first taste of the light ruby red wine, Laura inhales the gossamer aromas of red cherry, baking spice and toasty oak. She settles in to listen to this man with his iridescent green eyes and Scottish accent. He might be the most fascinating creatures she has met since her days at Vassar when she was madly in love with her poetry teacher *what was his name? Red Feather? Or something like that, he was a bit hokey, but he really believed he was a reincarnation of an Indian Chief. Perhaps too much peyote had fed his delusion.*

"What we are getting closer to doin', and I'm hopin' we will have a breakthrough this time, is we are using AI to map what Daisy sees and show it on a computer screen."

"Wow that is cutting edge." *How would he kiss her the first time? Gently or passionately?*

Laura starts searching for her phone. It is in one of her pockets, but she doesn't remember which one. She had felt self-conscious about laying it on the table like she normally might have, but finally locates it. "Let me show you something." She pulls up a black and white photograph of the Crescent with a huge ominous cloud handing over it.

"I saw that in the gift shop."

"Isn't it eerie?" she says wrinkling her nose. "There's a scientific explanation for the cloud formation, but to me it's a sign that there is something supernatural going on here."

"That's because it's visual. We are always more convinced when we can see something. That's why it's critical for us to provide somethin' visual with our AI app. People are skeptical of photography because of its ability to be manipulated. AI science is costly, that's why we are needin' to accept the television rights to this project."

"Oh, I thought that was still up in the air?"

"Not anymore, I wanted to talk to you about this tonight, because they want us to sign the contract and I need a contract with you to proceed."

Damn, I can't sign a contract tonight without Liam involved and I'm three sheets to the wind. "Well, I'll have to review it tomorrow when I'm at my desk."

"Of course. I did take the liberty of giving Liam a copy this morning."

Their soup arrives, Laura's favorite, a hearty lobster bisque. "I asked Chef Daniel to prepare four courses only. It wears me out to have too much food and of course I abhor wasting fine cuisine.

"Tod would you bring me a single glass of Pouilly-Fuisse white burgundy to go with this?" she asks before he disappears.

"Of course, is there anything else I can bring you right now?

"No, thanks." She picks up her phone again. "Excuse me, I need to see if we can get our lawyer to review the contract as well. It might take a few days to line him up, you understand?"

...Liam call David Baxter and get him to review contract Sean gave you this morning...

The dots on her phone bubble back, then halt.

...already on it...

"Good maybe we can meet tomorrow sometime," she tells Sean, "we'll let you know when."

"Great, I'd like to invite you to join our ghost discovery tonight."

"No… that would be fun but not tonight. Let's just enjoy this fine dinner."

Who You Gonna' Call?

Tumbling into bed Laura resolves to stay sober tomorrow and to do this she will need lots of exercise and work. *Work, work, work…got to pull this together, must meet this deadline.* She buries her head in Cloud's soft fur and pulls the pillows up around both of them making a nest of sorts while fantasizing about the handsome man in her hotel.

As Laura softly begins to snore Cloud pops his head up. *There she is, the girl with the child who is always crying.* Cloud growls low and fiercely, trying not to wake Laura up. *Get the hell out of here!* Seemingly startled and frightened by Cloud's growling, the apparition turns and flees.

Laura's phone wakes her from a deep sleep. "Yes, Liam what is it?"

I've got David coming over at 4:00 this afternoon to go over the contract with us. Does that work for you?"

"Sure, how is it going?"

"Well, they're working mostly late at night, and they've been pretty quiet so far. No one has complained."

"Great, see you then."

"Computer set an alarm for 3:50 p.m."

She pulls herself out of bed, throws down a couple of energy drinks to boost her until her latte comes and throws herself into work sitting cross-legged on the bed.

Laura writes:

My grandmother Woku, my mother's mother, is now my only trusted guide. She helps me to see and understand I must seek purpose, and live a full life filled with joy. She is resolute I should live each day without considering the past unless it is to be aware of dangers which affect my survival. It's easier to talk about living and accepting the joy, but my mind wanders to greater things yet unlived. For now, I have my dogs and my friends, mostly boys, whom I choose carefully for I have a desire to be a leader. I don't know where this intense desire comes from. My name is a clue to my future. My warrior father named me Aadya, which means beyond this point.

When the alarm goes off, Laura has still not dressed or showered. "SHIT!" She pulls off the t-shirt she had slept in and dials Liam. "I'll be there in five minutes. She can almost hear him rolling his eyes over the phone, although he is too proper ever to do this publicly.

"Want to come?" Laura asks Cloud. He gives her a big "woof." *Of course, I want to go.*

Laura considers a quick whiff of bourbon then decides against it. *I don't want to smell like booze at 4 o'clock in the afternoon.*

Cloud lays down beside Laura through the whole boring meeting while they hash out the "buts" and what "ifs." He licks his paws out of boredom and lays his head down on his left leg and closes his eyes. When the meeting is finally over, this Sean fellow that she has been making googoo eyes over asks Laura if she will join them tonight. "We have this one room that Daisy has been absolutely goin' wild over. We're not linked up with the tech in Palo Alto yet, but he's comin' up here in a few days to show us how to wire Daisy up. When that happens, this will all blow wide open!"

"Sure, I'd love to. Where and when?"

"Room 712, 2 a.m."

Hhmm that's not gonna' happen. "I'm usually asleep by then unless I pull an all-nighter."

Sean shrugs, "Suit yourself, but one of these nights you really ought to come watch. Bring your dog with you and we'll see if he is talented like Daisy."

Laura and Cloud get back to the penthouse and she orders a loaded cheeseburger to be delivered at 7p.m. *What the heck, maybe I'll go tonight.*

"Oh, and computer set an alarm for 1:30 a.m."

I have set an alarm for 1:30 a.m.

"Computer tell me what you know about ghost hunting."

According to an article in Wikipedia, ghost hunting is the process of investigating locations that are reported to be haunted by ghosts. Typically, a ghost-hunting team will attempt to collect evidence supporting the existence of paranormal activity. Ghost hunters use a variety of electronic devices, including EMF meters, digital thermometers, both handheld and static digital video cameras,

including thermographic and night vision cameras, as well as digital audio recorders. Other more traditional techniques are also used, such as conducting interviews and researching the history of allegedly haunted sites. Ghost hunters may also refer to themselves as "paranormal investigators."

Ghost hunting has been heavily criticized for its dismissal of the scientific method. No scientific study has ever been able to confirm the existence of ghosts.

Would you like to know more?

"Yes, tell me about their methods."

Ghost hunters use a variety of techniques and tools to investigate alleged paranormal activity. While there is no universal acceptance among ghost hunters of the following methodologies, a number of these are commonly used by ghost hunting groups.

- Still photography and video: using digital, night vision, infrared, and disposable cameras.
- EMF meter: to detect possibly unexplained fluctuations in electromagnetic fields.
- Tablet PC: to record data, audio, video and environmental fluctuations such as electromagnetic fields.
- Ambient temperature measurement: using thermographic cameras, thermal imaging cameras, infrared thermometers, and other infra-

red temperature sensors. All of these methods only measure surface temperature and not ambient temperature.

- Digital and analog audio recording: to capture any unexplained noises and electronic voice phenomena (EVPs), that may be interpreted as disembodied voices.
- Compass: some ghost hunters use a compass to determine the location of paranormal spots, similar to EMFs.
- Geiger counter: to measure fluctuations in radiation.
- Infrared and/or ultrasonic motion sensors: to detect possible anomalous movement within a given area, or to assist in creating a controlled environment where any human movement is detected.
- Air quality monitoring equipment: to assess the levels of gases such as carbon monoxide, which are thought to contribute to reports of paranormal activity.
- Infrasound monitoring equipment: to assess the level of sound vibrations.
- Dowsing rods: usually constructed of brass and bent into an L-shape.
- Psychics, mediums, or clairvoyants: trance mediums or "sensitive" individuals thought to have the ability to identify and make contact with spiritual entities.
- Demonologists, exorcists, and clergy: individuals who may say prayers, give blessings, or per-

form rituals for the purpose of cleansing a location of alleged ghosts, demons, poltergeists, or "negative energy".

- Lights out: according to ghost hunting enthusiast websites, many ghost hunters prefer to conduct their investigations during "peak" evening hours (midnight to 4 a.m.).
- Ghost Box: a radio with a frequency scan mode that some ghost hunters claim allows communication with spirits.
- Interviews: collecting testimony and accounts about alleged hauntings.
- Historical research: researching the history behind the site being investigated.
- A Ouija board to communicate with spirits.
- According to a psychic medium, "dogs growling and barking at certain places on a property" and cats gravitating or looking into a particular area as if someone were present are believed to indicate a haunting.

Would you like to know more?

"No, that's enough for now." *My God I had no idea there was that much to it.* Laura looks in the cabinet for something that would go well with a cheeseburger. She shrugs and goes to the fridge where there are several bottles of a local micro-brewery beer and pops one open.

Making a Mark

The alarm goes off and Laura bolts up. Her head is pounding. *Shit, it's the middle of the night!* Then she remembers why she had set the alarm in the first place. She slips on a hoodie and some yoga pants and heads out to her first ghost hunt. Cloud whines. "Oh, what the hell, Sean said to bring you."

Who better? I can actually see the spirits. "Whoof!" he tells her and wags his tail. *It's all I can do.*

When they arrive at room 712, one floor beneath Laura's penthouse, she turns the door handle carefully in an effort to not make any noise.

Holy Crap there's four of them in here all at once! Cloud growls softly, causing Daisy to trot up to him and tell him to follow her lead. There are cameras and people and computer screens everywhere in the darkness, but the ghostly figures appear clearly to only Cloud and Daisy. Daisy approaches the apparition of a small boy in shorts and a beanie cap and paws with her right front pad. She sits facing in the direction of the boy. The luminescent figure doesn't stay put for long, and she follows him around indicating his whereabouts with the repetitive actions. Two video cameras on tripods and several smart phones follow her every move. A weird looking woman in a skinny dress with fringe on it sits cowering in a chair in the corner and a large man paces the floor, wringing his baseball cap in his hand. The other ghost doesn't seem to belong with these three as she is a modestly dressed woman in a distinctively different style of clothing.

Daisy clearly has more than she can manage. Cloud takes her lead and goes over to the woman in the chair sitting resolutely as if his position might encourage the apparition to stay there. He whines to make sure everyone is aware of his participation.

Sean lights up with comprehension and, using hand signals, tells everyone that Cloud is marking as well. Meters come out and keyboards click. There is a new heightened tension in the air. This goes on for hours. Everyone is so pumped up they don't notice as the sun starts peeking through the heavy velvet curtains of the style from the last century.

Finally, Sean speaks. His slightly noticeable Scottish brogue still surprises Laura every time he says something. "Let's call it a night folks. Mark will be flyin' in today with the headgear for Daisy and hopefully he has worked out the bugs on the software."

Someone opens the curtains to see to pack up, and the ghostly images disappear in the bright light.

Sean looks at Cloud and then Laura. "Did you see him markin'? He can see the images too."

"That wouldn't surprise me, I've kind of thought that myself before."

"Come her pretty boy. Are you a ghost dog too?" Sensing Sean has real affection for him and is not just trying to impress Laura, Cloud abides the attention and trots over to Sean and allows him to scratch his ears.

The adrenaline is starting to wear off and Laura yawns a large and lingering yawn. She is ready to head upstairs. "Good night all," she says to the room.

"I'll call you later this afternoon Laura, we have much to talk about."

"Okay, sure." She is sleepy and doesn't get too excited over his suggestion. As she and Cloud walk upstairs the one flight, Laura decides to text the kitchen.

...no coffee or breakfast until after 11 a.m. then send Belgian waffles with strawberries and whipped cream. Please ring the bell until I answer...

Wired Up

...Laura you've got to see this...

It is a text from Sean. Who she didn't know had her number.

...What is it?...

...Mark has arrived with the AI equipment. It's broad daylight and we are seeing what Daisy sees...

...OMG I'll be right there. Where are you?...

...room 622...

When she gets there, Daisy is still adjusting to the head gear and is being kind of squirrely about it. Her handler, a young woman from Stanford, is talking her down and rewarding Daisy frequently with tidbits of treats.

"Come here and look at the screen," Sean pulls her by the hand. "I want you to meet Mark, the genius behind this software."

Mark from MIT is just a kid. *He doesn't look old enough to be in college.* There on the screen of Mark's laptop is the room full of people as Daisy sees it. Laura is rendered speechless as she takes in the blurry vision of the multiple apparitions around the room.

"We've already got a lot going on in here, we didn't expect to see any ghosts yet," Sean tells her. "We wanted to test drive the equipment. Tonight, will be the true test.

The kid looks up at her from his chair. "Dogs see better than we do in dim light, but they read red and green as the same." He explains as if she had asked him a question.

With the kid and Sean both galvanizing their technical aspirations out loud the mood is even more profane as they watch ghosts move about the room.

But then one of the ghosts does something peculiar. A man in a suit and old-fashioned ball cap does an impromptu, free-standing flip in the air. Silence thickens in the room like a gelatinous blob, heavy and suffocating.

"Shit!" Slides out of the kid's mouth and Laura feels her arm hair do a dance as chill bumps spread from the back of her neck down past her elbows. The same man grins and takes a bow for his peculiar audience laden with cumbersome equipment. He then grabs one of the ladies and begins dancing. His joy spreads to the others cast in blurry computer shadows and it is apparent they are performing for their astounded audience.

Daisy, not understanding that her headset is broadcasting the images on the computer screens, continues her pawing as she has been trained. Haley, Daisy's handler takes her over to one of the computer screens to expose her to what they are seeing and rewards her with treats. Daisy doesn't yet comprehend the sign language is unnecessary and keeps up her solitary game of charades.

The measure of time feels flawed and elusive as the energy on both ends of the time warp bubbles over anxiously, seeking the equilibrium of an agreed upon reality.

"I know you don't want to stop, Sean," Haley says, "but it is my responsibility to Daisy that we don't blow her out. She needs a break and some exercise."

Sean frowns. "I know."

He looks at his watch. "We'll reconvene at 10 p.m."

Hardly able to contain the adrenaline rush of the moment, Sean looks to Laura.

"Will you join us tonight? Laura, this is history in the makin'!"

Am I crazy or is he sending me signals? Ever since she had met the man, she'd had a crush on him. This is the first time she allows something might be reciprocated.

"Would you like to join me for dinner this evening before you get started working? Sort of a celebration of today's good news." The words are out before she has a chance to think them through.

His "sure" comes out almost as a question.

"I was thinking at my place this time. I'll go upstairs and cook all afternoon for you."

He looks even more puzzled.

"Just kidding. What's your favorite meal?

"Oh, I dunno. Why don't you surprise me?"

"Steak it is. That's Cloud's favorite meal. How about 7:00 is that early enough for you?

"Sure," he says with sort of a sucking sound first as if to mask his hesitation. "The crew can set up without me."

Signals

Chef Daniel sends up a couple of seasoned waiters to cater their meal and one of the junior chefs to grill the steaks out on her patio. *He has outdone himself again. We are fortunate to have that man on staff.* Liam recruited Chef from The Cliff House a couple of years ago and he had been a total blessing to the smooth operation of the hotel. Keeping Chef Daniel happy was another matter entirely. He was dreadfully expensive, and like many chefs, was a real ego maniac, but apparently Liam knew how to keep him happily employed at the Crescent.

"Just don't sleep with him," Liam had warned her." *Right Liam, no problem.* It had almost happened once, though he wasn't really her type.

Laura sips on one of the wines the staff has brought, and nibbles on some delicately flavored cheeses from the Cowgirl Creamery steering completely clear of bourbon. Sean doesn't drink and it will be another long night. She plans to nap after Sean leaves and get up at 1:30 again in order to see this crazy drama unfold.

Cloud paces. The tantalizing smells of the grill have him worked up. It's obvious company is coming because Laura has dressed up more than usual and he hasn't seen such a fuss made over dinner in a long time. *Damn it smells good!* Perhaps it is that fellow who came the other day with that cute black and white number. People didn't usually call on them and bring their dog, but he had. When the doorbell rings, Cloud jumps up on the couch, gives a warning "woof" and leaps down, trotting over to the door.

Bummer, no Daisy.

"Hi there," Laura leans over and hugs Sean as if she has been doing this for years.

He shyly hands her a bottle of wine, then looks around awkwardly seeing that all necessities have been provided for. "I asked one of the kids on the crew to pick this up for me."

"Of course, how very sweet of you. And you don't even drink yourself." *He could have brought me a bag of horse poop and nothing would detract from those beautiful eyes and sexy accent.*

"These guys will cook and serve and then they'll be on their way. It's a dire lifestyle, but somebody's got to live it."

"I understand your grandmother was a well-known madam in San Francisco," he says taking off his jacket. "Didn't she buy the hotel with her spoils and then went legit, even allowing some single mothers to stay here for free?"

"Oh, I see you've been studying the history of the hotel."

"Well, yes that's part of our work, unravelin' the mysteries of the ghost images we study.

"I'm not at all sure that ghosts are lost souls though. Through the years I have altered some of my opinions about why the apparitions are here."

"How so?"

"Well, I believe I shared with you a little bit about the latest quantum physics theories. Even Einstein made reference to alternate realities."

"Really?" She nods to one of the staff and points at Sean's hand, so as not to interrupt him. The waiter brings Sean a drink.

"Sorry to interrupt, this is a non-alcoholic Irish Rose. I think you'll like it."

"Oh, what's in it?"

"Lemon juice, cherry juice, soda water and mint leaves.

"Mmm, sounds delicious, sort of like a Shirley Temple?"

Laura experiences a hot flash of triggered adrenaline rise up uncontrollably into her cheeks. "They told me that's what you've been ordering at the bar."

"It is, and now I am teasin' you." He flashes a reassuring smile and moves on realizing he has really embarrassed her.

"Anyway, what were we talking about? "Quantum physics," he relaxes his shoulders a bit. "I hardly understand it myself. I do have some interesting news though," he says changing the subject." We have caught wind of a 26-year-old speech pathologist that has taught her dog how to talk by usin' a custom sound board she has developed."

"Really? You've got to wonder what has taken them so long. It was like 30 years ago when they started teaching gorillas to sign."

Sean shrugs. "You're right. What *has* taken them so long?" He asks overly serious.

"Will you have her train Daisy?"

"Not sure yet, Daisy is already articulate with her body language. And dependin' on our success with the brain imaging, we might not need it. We'll have to see. There might be some nuances we could capture with trainin' like that, but I don't know yet."

The waiters signal to Laura to let her know they need to be seated. They have placed an antique lace tablecloth on her dining table, a crystal vase filled with yellow roses and set the table with silver from Laura's buffet. Next, they bring a divine bouillabaisse with a bit of a spicy kick. With the veranda doors open Laura and Sean can smell and hear the steaks sizzling on the grill.

Laura signals for more wine and by the end of their meal of Scottish Salmon Oscar, a crisp spinach salad, grilled asparagus, paper thin potatoes baked in cheese, and of course, the freshly grilled Kansas City Strip steak, she is so full she's not sure she can walk. She cuts up most of her steak and feeds it to Cloud, who is more than capable of making it disappear. He sits politely at her side insuring he will not miss the opportunities of each morsel. Laura watches Sean enjoy the strawberry shortcake which she can only wave away. "Please stick it in the refrigerator and I'll eat it for breakfast. *Sure would like to pass on the late-night adventure, but it is clear Sean wants me there.*

Laura walks Sean to the door politely and surprising her, he kisses her goodbye discreetly at the door as the staff cleans up the kitchen. *Mmm...now this could get interesting.*

Progress

It is more of a struggle to rise in the middle of the night than Laura has anticipated. *But, oh my God, look at those images on the screen. It's unreal.*

Everyone in the room is staring at Mark's computer screen and palpable awe and shock is on every face.

They have allowed a few of the ghost tour crew into the room, and some other guy she can't identify. There are three ghostly female figures and a cat, of all things. Sean is completely absorbed by what he sees that he hardly notices her. He glances up briefly, but a smile is all she gets as the apparitions move around the room, some more quickly than others.

One of the female ghosts picks up the cat and it is looking like she is listening to him purr.

Everyone is the room is hypnotized by the miracles taking place. It takes the sunshine, breaking through some low-level clouds, and streaking nervously past the pulled drapes to break the spell.

Daisy is starting to paw at her headgear and Sean intervenes by declaring it is time to pack it up and let everyone rest.

"Nobel prize." is all he says grinning to Mark who has now taken the sobriquet "Mark the Magician."

After last night's victorious breakthrough Laura realizes she will be challenged to stay up all night and continue the progress made on her book. *At least today has been productive.* Despite waking up to Sean's distraught phone call just before noon.

"Laura, the news media have caught wind of this, and it's an absolute nightmare. Mark has shut down all correspondence with the outside world to protect his scientific discovery, but apparently there have been some leaks. I have instructed Liam to have a staff meeting and make everyone sign an NDA. I didn't anticipate how viral this was goin' to go."

"Whatever you need to do is fine with me," she says, calmly managing her own panic. Supposedly there is no such thing as bad publicity. *Even so the hotel is my sanctuary.* The thought of facing an onslaught of curiosity seekers makes her stomach roil.

"Laura,"

"Yes."

"I really appreciate the dinner last night."

So that was a kiss and not my imagination. "Well, I was trying to impress you with all my cooking skills."

"I'd like to see you again soon, but I do feel swamped by these, well, amazing events. This is the culmination of my life's work."

She was stone cold sober, hadn't had anything to drink since last night and the words he uttered made her feel as light-headed as if someone had switched off her oxygen

"Are you there?"

"Yes, of course, I was just thinking."

"What were you thinkin'?"

"Well, I would like to see you again too, but how do we make that happen?"

"I tell you what, give me a couple more days to get this crew back into a routine, let the mayhem die down, and I'll take you out to dinner…Maybe we can go next Friday night."

"Sounds good to me."

"In the meantime, please come to the tracking we are doing."

"You know it is both fascinating and creepy to be able to see those ghosts. I live here, you know."

"Laura,"

"Yes."

"I've got some limited information on your grandmother, but I'd like some more if you have any personal information that could be helpful. While the images are somewhat fuzzy, we are beginnin' to think the apparitions may be from separate times based on the clothing styles."

"Hmm, I'll look into that. I vaguely remember some papers lying around somewhere."

Laura hangs up, feeling an urgency to get back to writing where she has control of the outcome. These otherworldly disruptions in her life, while exciting, leave her on edge and the only remedies are drinking and writing. The first solution becoming trickier but still enjoyable, and the latter being life affirming. *Got to control my weight, got to control my drinking.*

"Computer, how many manuscript pages in my 'Work in Progress' file?"

There are 185 pages in the Work in Progress file.

Laura looks out the window of her office where she can see the deep-set blue of the Bay below. The view is a ticket to inspiration that she never takes for granted.

Treasure Trove

...I'm in one of the attic spaces on the 8th floor and I've found a treasure trove of letters and photographs of my grandmother and some of the women who stayed here after having babies...

The dots bubble as Sean writes back.

...totally cool... can I look at them later? I'm meeting with the crew right now...

...Sure, but I think you will want to analyze this room. It feels creepy...

... Is Cloud with you?...

...Yes, and he has been whining a lot...

...I'll talk to you in a little while...

...k...

Laura looks around the space plastered in wayward spider webs and decades of dust. There is one window in the mansard roof facing the city which lets in a beam of natural light. Other than that, there is a single bulb and chain powered by old-knob-and-tube wiring that has never been changed out. Laura has found a trunk full of letters, postcards, and pictures. Several exotic burlesque costumes hang in a corner on a makeshift rod. Their glamor, from another era, is constructed with lace and shiny sequins carefully crafted into textile secrets and curves of lust. Laura has not allowed the ghost tour crew to use these artifacts as they were personal to her grandmother. Through the years of neglect, some items have been gnawed on by rodents of varying sizes, and other items have disappeared into obscurity for no apparent reason. She has brought Cloud with her for moral support. Still, there is a sense of vulnerability that washes over her here in this fetid room.

"Come on, Cloud, let's get out of here."

I thought you would never ask. He hops up on all fours and shakes. His beautiful white coat has been tarnished by the dust of the attic floor and the rotting smells have attached themselves to his fur. *The old woman sitting in the rocker hasn't moved once until now.* As a parting gesture she winks at Cloud with a puckish smile and blows him a kiss while twisting the rocker and causing it to knock a book on the floor. Laura jumps.

What the hell! Laura looks down at the book bound in leather and picks it up. It is her grandmother's diary and accounting of visitors to her original house of ill repute on Maiden Street. She picks it up hastily and rushes out the door.

Score

"What a scoor Laura!"

The way he pronounces score makes her salivate.

"I thought you would be pleased," she tells Sean who is sitting with her on the couch close enough their thighs touch. She is sipping on a tart Chablis which is taking off the creepy feeling she has had since this morning when she and Cloud had gone into the attic. The afternoon sun slanting through the tall windows of her living room adds to her mellow. She wants to lean over and kiss Sean, but the moment has not yet occurred.

"I'd like to look at all of the things you found."

"I was thinking I could get a cleaning crew up there and bring everything down."

"Oh no, especially with what you are telling me about how the book surfaced. I think we have a grand opportunity here.

"I'd like to set up a crew in there before everything is disturbed. Then I can have Judy, who does all my research, catalog everything once we have had a chance to film in there."

All right already! Are these two going to talk all day or are they going to go after it? Cloud jumps up on the couch crazed by all the pheromones in the room. He decides to take drastic action by awkwardly sitting on Sean, who has *got to be the slowest player in the history of mankind.* The unsettling commotion knocks Sean off balance and he inadvertently slumps in the plush cushions toward Laura. They are laughing and he is now too close not to kiss her, and then it happens, a deep, tongue-plunging movie star kiss. And his hands are on her breasts before anyone can identify what is happening.

Mission accomplished. Cloud jumps down and makes himself scarce.

Laura lets the Chablis mellow dictate her response. Perhaps fearful she is going to spill the wine on him, Sean takes her glass and sets it on the side table. This doesn't keep him from moving the action forward as he pulls his shirt over his head and proceeds to tackle the buttons of her pearly silk blouse.

The window-filtered radiant sun tickles as her bare skin is released to its touch. Her nipples are on fire as she succumbs to his grasp, and the sexual tension that has been building since she first laid eyes on him weeks ago in New York is allowed out of its cage.

"I've got to tell you," he says sitting up after they are done, "I haven't been sober long, and your drinking scares me."

ZING! As in that was absolutely fucking amazing. Do *we really have to talk about this right now?* Leaning against the big round arm of the couch Laura picks up her wine-glass and clutches it to her breasts, as if for protection from whatever Sean is going to say next. She swallows the wine and lets the liquid gold flow slowly down the back of her throat. Perhaps this is her answer because she can't think of anything to say.

And he stares at her as if waiting for some promise of cooperation—she has nothing to offer. Instead she gives him a lewd invitation with her body, robbing him of any opportunity to resist. His boyish grin spans across his face and they go after it again.

Geesh I've unleashed a monster. Now they won't stop. Cloud scratches at his nose with his paw in that endearing way Laura adores, but she is too absorbed in Sean to notice.

Afterwards, Laura is ready for Sean to leave so she goes into the shower where he joins her and continues the erotic play with a bar of soap. Realizing she's not into it, they both rinse off.

Darkness is now creeping through the tall, hand-rolled glass windows and Laura watches as he pulls on his pants. She pours another glass of the chilled Chablis, not feeling conversational and ready for him to leave.

"I know you're not a late-night person, but you have to come to that attic space tonight with the crew. If your grandmother is there, we can see her with Daisy's headgear."

"No, I get it. I'll be there."

"This is all so freakin' amazin', Laura!"

She smiles at him with as much enthusiasm as she can muster and shuts the door behind him.

Nanu

Laura stops typing and takes a sip of coffee. She has been writing non-stop since 3 o'clock after she took Cloud on his afternoon walk and it is nearly 9 o'clock now. She has forgotten to eat dinner, and more importantly she has skipped the cocktail hour. *Definitely time to quit!*

"Computer, what information do you have on my grandmother Elizabeth Schuster of San Francisco?"

Elizabeth Schuster ran one of San Francisco's more notorious brothels. She arrived in the San Francisco area in 1936 from Charleston, South Carolina, after having been seduced by an older man who abandoned her when she got pregnant. After she lost the baby in childbirth, Schuster traveled to San Francisco on a dare. Working as a waitress and living in a boarding house, she soon found herself guiding young women into making more money by becoming prostitutes. Her skill at managing people and money soon led her to open the house of ill repute known affectionately by customers as the "meat market." Politicians, prominent businessmen, and even world leaders were known to conduct business in the living room of the mansion on Maiden Street. In her late 60s, Schuster, affectionately known as Sally, had a change of heart. She sold her "Little Black Book" for $20,000 dollars to an up-and-coming madam, and used her savings to buy the Crescent Hotel on Nob Hill where she often hosted young, pregnant women for as long as

they needed to get back on their feet. "Sally," died in her 80s. leaving her hotel and small fortune to her granddaughter, Laura Haskell, a noted author of fantasy fiction.

It was Laura's first time to actually research her grandmother. *You've got to wonder how many kids have grandmothers who used to be madams?*

Laura had been told as a teenager that Grandmother Elizabeth, or Nanu, had once been involved in shady business dealings, but the topic was so sacrosanct she hadn't explored it much until her grandmother took her on a memorable trip to Europe for her college graduation present. They became close and that's when Laura learned first-hand about where her Grandmother's fortune had come from.

At that time the illustrious old broad was on the downside of 70 and had looked, if anything, proper and matriarchal with her chunky oversized pearl strand and a cream-colored Gucci business suit when she showed up at Laura's graduation from Vassar, her mother's alma mater as well. After that trip, when Nanu had pronounced Laura should be the heir of the Crescent Hotel, was when Laura began to write in earnest, knowing money wasn't going to be an issue for her going forward. Nanu's death, and Laura's subsequent inheritance event, occurred as Laura was going through her divorce from John, the financier, and it seemed like the perfect excuse to get out of Boston.

For the most part, Laura's childhood was relatively normal. Growing up in Virginia, her parents had been successful in their own rights. Both Ivy League-educated lawyers, her parents had eschewed the D.C. scene and had chosen to raise their only daughter in Falls Church, a safe and well-heeled environment.

Laura's mother, Emily, had no memory of the house on Maiden Street. She had been raised by an aunt and uncle starting at the age of three, until she was old enough to be shipped off to several of the country's most posh boarding schools. This caused her to entirely skip the whole flower power generation that was happening in the '60's. *One of the most electrifying times in American history, post 1900, and my mother had been boxed into conventionalism while Nanu was busy tying up the loose ends of her licentious career.*

Laura's grandfather was supposedly a prominent politician who had agreed to father "Sally's" child only if his identity were never revealed. Nanu stayed faithful to his desire and took his secret to her grave. Laura's mother was considerably bitter at the time that not only was her mother a famous madam, but would not reveal her father's identity to her. Emily had accused Nanu, whom she called Elizabeth and not mother, of being a heartless bitch right there in the hospital as she lay dying.

"Why did you even have a child?" Emily had shrieked, her cold controlled lawyer's anger abandoned by the circumstances. Nanu was merely a breathing corpse at that point. *So cruel of her, but excusable under the circumstances.*

Nanu had smiled at her daughter and granddaughter with devilish eyes. "The truth is we loved each other and you two were my only legacy to this life that I could cherish and be proud of."

While her mother choked down expletives, it was Laura who leaned in to Nanu taking her hand and kissing it—as vulnerable to Sally's mysterious ability to assimilate the identity needed for the beholder as her past Johns were. With salty tears further clouding her vision, Laura watched as her Nanu faded away, dying hours later.

Research

Cloud whines, bringing Laura back to reality. "Come on sweetie, I'll take you down for last call."

As it happens, they run into Judy in the lobby. She is plugged into her phone via earbuds listening to something intently, and slouched down into one of the overstuffed leather chairs. Laura decides to sneak past her, but when she returns from the walk, changes her mind and does stop to engage.

"Have you had any luck finding info on my grandmother?" Laura has to practically poke Judy to get her attention.

"Oh hi, Laura, what was that?" Judy says pulling out her earbuds.

"I said, have you found any info on my Grandmother, Elizabeth Schuster?"

Judy stands up and tugs at her shirt. "Yes, actually. She was included in two different books I have come across."

"Oh great, I don't have much myself, yet. I just know there is a treasure trove in that one attic room."

"Yes, they are setting up in there as we speak."

Damn this late-night business is getting old, but I don't want to miss it if they see Nanu.

"I guess I'd better be there tonight. I'll see you guys after a while."

Burlesque Queen

When they get back to the apartment, Laura opens a bottle of champagne and sits down on the couch with Cloud to watch a movie on FilmFlix. Soon she is snoring, only to be awoken by Cloud who is pawing her arm with his scratchy pads. She notices the bottle is mostly empty.

Wake up little Suzy! You didn't set the alarm and the night is getting away from us.

"Leave me alone Cloud! Go away."

Nope, they're expecting us and I'm going with you. He barks forcefully to get her attention.

"Cloud leave me be!"

But then her phone rings. She leans over to grab her cell off the overstuffed armrest of the couch. It is emitting an irreverently harsh beacon of light. "What the hell? Who would be calling me this late?"

It's Sean. "Laura, we need you up here. You won't believe your eyes. We are in the attic space with your Grandmother's things and we think it's your grandmother here, dressed like a burlesque dancer and she has been performin' an exotic dance for a man in a business suit."

Laura giggles. *What could be more ludicrous than this phone call in the middle of the night?* "I'm sorry if I didn't know better, I'd say you've been drinking. What makes you think it is Elizabeth?"

"With Daisy's vision screen we can see her rather well, she's been makin' motions like she is trying to identify herself to us, like pointin' at the journals and pretendin' to write on her palm. Judy has seen pictures of her, and also thinks it's your grandmother."

Laura straightens up and sparks of cognitive function blast through her mental fog like pressurized water dousing a fire. "Oh okay, I've been writing all night," she lies, "and the time got away from me." For the first time she notices her resentment toward Sean because he doesn't drink.

Laura looks at the mirror and decides not to change out of her sweats, because she is just going down the hall. She pulls at her rumpled hair and blows that off too. *It will be dark, no one will notice my slovenliness.*

Cloud slips out the door of the suite at her side so deftly there is no fighting that either. His nose puckers up almost involuntarily. The air has that peculiar electrical smell he often notices when the apparitions are around. As Laura slowly opens the door to the attic space, Cloud pushes through the door and sees what Sean was describing to her on the phone. *Holy mother of God! That woman is practically sticking it in his face.*

But as Laura enters the room behind Cloud everything changes. The eerie vibes of the attic space she had visited a few days before are gone now that the area is packed with crew and their high-tech computer screens and meters. Most importantly, she misses out entirely on the hypnotizing 'show' everyone is glued to until the instant she walked in. The woman and man are swallowed up like a flash of lightening in reverse. Everything goes black, but no one flinches in this game of 'who can see the ghost,' all except for one of the camera operators who sniffles once or twice. Sean is unable to disguise his disdain as he glares at Laura with the disappointment of someone who has discovered their ice cream sundae has been served without nuts.

"Tell me you got all that recorded," he says in a hushed tone turning toward Mark.

Laura has woken up enough now to regret her fashion choices, while Sean points to a chair he has had brought in for her nearby the AI screen. Cloud settles in next to her.

Sean throws up his arms with angst. "I don't know what happened. She was really performin' for us, and that other ghost was there too."

"Show me the playback," Laura tells Mark. What she sees is disarming. The erotic dancer does look like a young version of her grandmother Elizabeth, or to the family known as Nanu.

"Freeze it so I can get a good look at that man." In her half-dazed mental state, Laura hopes the apparition might hold the answer to the frustrating mystery of who her grandfather was.

"Do you know who he is?" Sean asks her.

"Nope, put Judy on it though. She'll find out."

Then as suddenly as they two ghosts disappear, another appears. It is a much older version of Elizabeth and dressed in a way Laura would recognize her. "That's her! That's my grandmother." The apparition smiles purposefully at Laura. Chills ripple down her spine, wrenching reality into little pieces and crushing Laura's ability to discern the real from the imagined.

Cloud growls softly with protection for Laura, smelling her body's chemical changes. He rubs up against her, pushing a little. It is this action, and the touch of his feathery coat that brings her back into the physical space of the room. She strokes his back and feels his ribs as she stares at the computer screen revealing her grandmother. Each person in the room is dealing with their own astonishment, and the shared silence is cloaking the rising pulses, the blood pressure booming, and the sheer agony of their complicit discovery.

"Nanu, we can see you!" Laura says reflexively to her grandmother's presence.

"Who was that man?" Her brain is starting to fire, recognizing the immediacy at hand.

Exasperatingly, Nanu shrugs and acts frustrated. She flays her hands toward the books and magazines piled on the floor. Again, she sits in the rocker, but this time she lets it rock gently back and forth.

"Did you feel that?" someone in the room asks. There is an undercurrent of murmuring.

"Sean, the temperature has dropped five degrees in the last three minutes," someone else reports. Cloud's ruff is extended like spikey horns on his spine as he watches the antics of Nanu. Then suddenly, nothing. She disappears again the same way she did previously like her image sucked back into a vacuum.

"Hold steady everyone, she'll be back." Sean advises. Everyone waits almost completely still for several minutes; the shuffling of feet and the sounds of whispering indicate the crew is starting to get restless.

"What's the time?" asks a crewmember over in the corner.

"2:30 a.m." another replies. They continue to wait as it becomes apparent there will be no more apparitions for tonight.

I guess these guys don't get it. She's not coming back. Cloud pushes against Laura's leg and barks. The crew looks at him stunned. Daisy starts to rub off her headset and everyone laughs.

"I guess they're trying to tell us something," Judy says.

"Okay, let's pack it up for the night, guys. Thank you everyone.

"I'd like us all to meet at 2 o'clock in the conservatory for a brainstormin' session. Do your analysis before then. Let's not waste our time."

"Judy, I want to find out who that man was, and I want to hear ideas about what you guys think happened."

Laura was going to slink out, but Sean grabs her hand. He looks as if he is going to say something consequential, then stops short.

"See you tomorrow?" Is all he says.

"Sure." She answers

"We're still on for Friday…dinner?"

"Of course."

"There are only a few more days of filming here, then we head for Spain."

"Oh?" *That must have been what he wanted to tell her.*

"I thought you would be here longer, based on all the progress you've made."

"I know, it would be nice, but we run on a schedule. And now that FilmFlix is involved, we have to stick to it."

Possibilities

Turns out the male apparition in the attic resembles Michael Lewinsky, the Attorney General of the State of California who held office for eight years, about the time Laura's mother would have been conceived.

As a courtesy Judy calls Laura to let her know. "Yes, I'm awake."

"I have some compelling evidence who your grandfather was. Can I come by and show you what I have?"

"Give me 30 minutes, would you?"

"Sure, I wanted to meet with you before I shared this with the crew."

"I appreciate that."

Laura can feel her blood pressure soaring and yet she still texts the kitchen to send up a couple of lattes. *If this is real, mother will shit a brick!*

Showering usually calmed her, but not today. To not know exactly who you come from presents an uncertain rawness. *Like something orphans must experience. It was especially difficult for mother, who had sought respectability at every turn.* Nanu's legacy was difficult enough to reconcile, but not knowing the other half of the equation had been debilitating at certain points in Laura's life too.

Laura answers the door. "Come in Judy, long time no see."

"Well like I said, we're supposed to meet this afternoon, and this is such a private matter, under the circumstances, Sean and I both thought you should hear it straight from me first."

The kid from the kitchen with the lattes arrives before Laura closes the door.

"I know it's lazy not to make the coffee myself, but it's way too convenient to get someone else to do it." She shrugs, "just call me a princess."

"Oh, no judgement here," Judy waves her palm in front of her the way some people do in a round circular motion like they are cleaning a window. "I would do the same if I could. It was thoughtful to send for coffee."

Sitting down on the sofa next to Cloud Laura asks, "So what do you have? And how definitive do you think it is?"

"Well, cross referencing it with your grandmother's records, I have my money on Michael Lewinsky, but of course, I have more digging to do."

Laura clasps her chest and takes a deep breath. Cloud sits up and notices Laura's aura has completely changed colors.

"What leads you to this conclusion?"

"Well, he was frequently listed as a participant in meetings that took place at the house, but never listed as a client."

"That doesn't make sense."

"From what I've read about the Bradley Mansion on Maiden Street, it was often a meeting place for unofficial liaisons. Yes, it was a whore house, but it was also a place of great confidentiality where men were at ease to be themselves and talk frankly without looking over their shoulder. It had the mystique of 'Bro' code that filtered through all elements of conversation," Judy explains. "Then there are the diary entries…"

"Yes, let me see them. Do you have them with you?"

"Here" Judy slides the journal over to Laura,

"Mmm, this is good" Judy says sipping from her frothy drink. "How did you know how I like my coffee?"

Laura smiles, "Another advantage to ordering from the kitchen. I asked them to send up what you've been ordering for yourself.

"So, why would these men talk confidentially in front of call girls?" Laura asks.

"Well, apparently there was the 'board room.' Meals and refreshments could be sent in for longer meetings. No call girls were allowed in the room, except for a few women that were more like special executive escorts. They made so much money they wouldn't dare jeopardize their employment."

"I may be jumping ahead a bit, but now that we have DNA testing wouldn't it be easy enough to prove it? Laura sets her coffee down on the massive, burled redwood coffee table. "Are there any living descendants from, what's his name, Michael?

"Lewinsky"

"Oh my God, any relation to Monica?"

Judy giggles, "Don't think so, wouldn't that be a hoot?"

Picking her coffee back up, Laura understands the pressure of not knowing one's origins and how that void can slip away incrementally like a fault line moves to release. "Oh God, I've always wanted to know..."

With visibly shaking hands Laura looks at Judy. "Well, go ahead and share your info with the group. To find this out by ghost, well it's unreal."

"Can you do me a favor?" Laura asks.

"Sure."

"Once you've completed your thesis of sorts, could you write it up and let me have a copy?"

"Well, of course, it might take a while."

"I know, you're a busy gal." Laura stands up. "Now if you'll excuse me, I would like to make it to that meeting this afternoon myself and I have a bunch of things to do before then."

...met with Judy my head is spinning. Can you come by? I'll have some lunch delivered for us...

Sean texts back

...finishing my run now see you in 30...

...perfect...

Nooner

Laura pours a swig of bourbon into one of the heavy crystal highball glasses on her bar. She holds the fiery liquid in her mouth swishing it around with her tongue to experience the full exposure and bite of the booze. Then she allows it to slowly drain down her throat for the whiskey thrill she so desires.

Though it is still chilly, and the fog has not broken, she goes out onto the small veranda to finish the bourbon in her glass. Cloud follows her and pushes his face against her leg.

"I know sweetie. I have to think a minute," she tells him, grabbing at his ruff and affectionately pulling at him.

When the doorbell rings, Laura forgets about the several swigs of bourbon she has had and kisses Sean, then immediately regrets her transgression.

"Have a seat." Laura picks up the remote and punches the fireplace on. The gas logs burst into flames with a dull gas explosion.

"There's some cheese soup and Rueben sandwiches in the kitchen. Help yourself."

"Aren't you eatin'?"

"Yes, in a minute."

"Are you okay?" he asks grabbing her arms.

"Yes," she lets her head droop like a teenager, afraid to look him in the eyes.

Sean drops his hands and goes into the kitchen to get himself some lunch. "Where are the glasses?"

"I'm coming, let me help you."

"Just tell me where they are." He sounds a tad irritated.

"No, I'm sorry, you don't know anything about my kitchen. Here." She opens up the cabinet. There are no glasses. "I guess they are in the dishwasher."

"So, all this craziness… Judy thinks she has identified your grandfather." Sean says changing the subject.

"I know, right? If I tell my mother how we discovered him, she will definitely live up to her threats and put me in treatment."

Sean stops pouring his Perrier and looks straight at Laura. "She's threatened to do that?"

Laura laughs, "It's just a joke, Sean, chill out."

They sit on the couch to eat and watch the fire, while Laura tells Sean about growing up with a grandmother who was madam and a mother who answered to ma'am.

"How long before you have to be at your meeting?"

Sean checks his phone. "I have a little over an hour."

"Great!" she starts to unbutton his shirt and he doesn't resist. "We have time for a quickie."

As soon as Sean leaves, Laura experiences a sense of relief. *The sex is great, but I'm not getting attached to this guy and follow him around the world chasing ghosts.* Ever since her divorce, her only commitment has been to not be committed. Tonight, she and Sean are supposed to go out. They will all pack up and leave on Sunday.

…Liam, can you make it to the ghostbusters meeting at two? I'm running behind…

...Not sure I can squeeze it in, but I'll try...

...great, fill me in later...

What?

Say that again, you want me to do what?"

It's Friday night and Sean and Laura are on their dinner date. He has chosen to take her to The Boulevard, a swanky place next to the Embarcadero with a view of the Bay Bridge and the water.

"Well, if we could link you genetically to this Michael Lewinsky, we would have empirical evidence that our apparitions are real, that they lived here on this earth and that what we are doin' has scientific validity to it."

"You want me to take a DNA test and compare it to Lewinsky's living daughter's DNA?"

"It would be completely anonymous. We are just going to tell her that our client has requested us to do this. We'll tell a partial truth. Lewinsky was married to someone else before he was married to his wife of 40 years. And we'll say that the possible half-sister never knew her father and was unsure if her mother wasn't lyin' about who he was. We'll let his daughter sign a release from all consequences should we have located her half-sister, so she won't have anythin' to worry about, you know like someone wantin' a kidney from her or something like that. Or inheritance, that's a big issue."

"I'm not sure exactly how this proves your ghosts were real people, but it makes a great story and my mother certainly deserves to know who her father was."

"Exactly."

"Do you think you can pull this off?"

"My staff certainly can."

"What about if Lewinsky's daughter wants to know her half-sibling?"

"We'll deal with that if it becomes an issue."

"Genetic searches are common now and cheap, everybody's into genealogy.

I think our premise will fly."

Laura leans over and pours herself another glass of the full-bodied red cab she is drinking. The perfectly cooked petite filet she has just polished off is still settling into her stomach. She pushes the rest of the potato left on her plate around with her fork, then lays it down.

"I don't think I will say anything to my mother until we know the results."

"I wouldn't."

Laura looks at him and asks. "You've got a couple more days, then you're out of here?"

"Yes, we leave for Spain next without even letting any of the crew take a break. We have to stay out in front of this whole AI situation. I may not come up to breathe for months to come."

"That's too bad, I've enjoyed having you around, Sean. You are a very nice man."

"Ooh, yoo jus' like mae oversized cock," he says laying on his Scottish accent.

"Well, that too," she laughs. It is a joke, there is nothing abnormal about Sean's physique.

"I tell you what, after we go to Spain, we go to Croatia, then Italy, maybe you could come visit the jobsite in Italy, it's supposedly a huge villa on Lake Como."

He grabs her hand and presses his agenda, pinning her with his hypnotic green eyes. Her resolve fades like a cheap Madras print. "Sounds tempting. Maybe."

When they get back to the Crescent, Cloud is sprawled across Laura's huge bed as if staking claim to the whole territory of the kingdom of sleep. When she turns on the lights it spooks Cloud and his body twists comically as he leaps to all fours.

"Sorry, kiddo. Didn't mean to startle you."

"Just going to get a little night cap," she tells Sean, "and then I'll come to bed."

She could tell he is trying not to frown, but it's there on his face. *This would never work. Enjoy what you've got tonight.* And she goes to the bar to pour some pricey brandy into a crystal snifter.

Goodbye

Saying good-bye to Sean is more difficult than Laura anticipates. Ever since their date on Friday night they had taken every opportunity to be together. *I thought I had kept my shields up. Maybe not. Maybe meeting him in Italy in a couple months isn't such a bad idea after all. I could use a break and Italy in the Spring with a beautiful man, albeit busy man, sounds pretty tempting.*

There was still the pressure of not drinking, which did surface more than once. She had said something about cutting back, and he had pointedly told her, "It's not just another diet. Controlled drinking will only work for a short while, if at all. You will be miserable. Believe me I tried everything. It takes effort and help, but once you get some serious sobriety under your belt, your life will only continue to get better and better."

She asks him to come up to her suite to say good-bye before leaving. She doesn't want to be seen sending him off. Everyone at the hotel has bonded with the crew in the 10 days they have been there, as they have become an integral part of hotel life. Laura and Sean's romance is not the only one to emerge.

The doorbell rings and uncharacteristically Cloud trots over and pulls down on the hand lever Laura installed for him several years ago. "I guess he knew it was you," she laughs at a startled Sean looking at her from the other side of the room.

Cloud jumps up to hug him. *Damn I'm going to miss this guy. He's the only one that has ever been around who can mellow my girl out.* Frustrated he cannot tell Sean this; Cloud whines and licks his beard.

"Hello laddie," He embraces Cloud, still standing on his hind two legs and rubs his shoulders vigorously. "I'm going to miss you too, Cloud."

"What about me?" Laura goes to greet him.

He hugs her tightly and kisses her purposefully. "You, I'm going to pine for, until you come and see me."

"Can you sit a minute?"

He looks at his phone nervously. "I've been told I have 15 minutes max, before we jettison out of here for the airport."

"There are a few things I wanted to go over with you before I leave, though," he says nervously hanging near the door.

"Judy is working on our grand scheme to identify your grandfather. Someone will send you a DNA swab kit in the next couple of days. So, please follow through on that.

"And down the road we'll schedule another study here. I think there is much more to the story that we've left untouched. That grandmother of yours is such a rascal. She never stops amazin' us."

"You can't imagine how bizarre these conversations are, can you? Laura grins.

With eyes turned directly at her, he agrees. "No, I guess I cannot. And you can't begin to understand after a lifetime of chasin' ghosts, I've finally caught them."

"I'm happy for you, and I hope that you get the recognition and wealth you so richly deserve."

He clears his throat, and she is heavy with his departure.

"Goodbye Laura."

"Bye Sean." She watches him traverse down the hallway. *Will he do the little charming turnaround and gratuitous smile?* She waits for it, but he doesn't turn, and that's when she realizes she is in trouble because he is as downcast as she is.

Chocolate Soufflé

Laura spends the next three days in her pajamas, drinking and struggling with rationalizing not drinking, watching bad movies and smoking pot until it runs out. She eats salty junk food then pukes it up. She doesn't bother writing because, *it will just be crap.* Cloud has seen this before and so has Dusty, so have all her Crescent crew. Dusty doesn't wait for Laura to call, but uses his pass key to take care of Cloud as it is clear she has gone AWOL. She doesn't even notice when he and Cloud come and go.

Cloud paces, he lays down, he paces more, and occasionally he barks at her. He is so upset he throws up his high-dollar, canned dog food on the oriental rug, but nothing gets her attention. She continues to lift her glass and juggle her intermittent bursts of reality with sweet talk to him; asking forgiveness and telling him that she will soon get dressed and take him outside. He gnaws gently on her fingers if she dozes off for too long and is hypervigilant to observe her breathing. *She is slowly killing herself and there is nothing I can do.*

Nanu pays a visit and Cloud growls at her shadowy figure because she is unable to do anything like cook some chicken soup *or talk some sense into the girl for God's sake.* Nanu is not chased off by Cloud and lingers there with her granddaughter as the days tick by. Cloud watches Nanu tenderly caress her granddaughter, who is puddled into a mass of boozy stench.

Finally abandoning her ordeal, Laura orders a chocolate soufflé sent up and Liam builds up enough courage to confront her.

Delivering the soufflé personally, he launches into his rehearsed diatribe.

"You have absolutely got to stop this! You are killing yourself. And I won't have it."

Laura gives him a woozy smile and takes the soufflé from his hands. "Very endearing, my friend. Would you like a bite?" she goes into the kitchen and pulls out two spoons. She is wearing lemon-colored silk pajama bottoms, a Vassar T-shirt, and a plaid flannel robe.

"Laura, listen to me. You need help."

She rolls her eyes at him.

"I want to take you to an AA meeting."

"Did Sean put you up to this?"

"No."

"Then what's your problem?"

"You are my problem."

"I suppose I am," she says with a burst of honesty. "Why on earth would I want to go to an AA meeting?" she asks with unfettered snarkiness.

"It's either that or I call your father and mother."

She giggles, "Now that's the first funny thing you've said."

"I mean it. You are out of control."

"If you're not going to help me eat this thing," she points at the righteously delectable souffle she is hovering over, "then you probably should go."

"I'm holding you accountable." He points his finger at her for emphasis, but his action is wasted.

It won't be for another two days, when Dusty finds her lying on the floor, in her own vomit, that the paramedics are called to revive her.

It is there in the hospital away from her Miss Havisham existence that a doctor is able to deliver a message she can hear. He makes a deal with her to let him pick her up and go to a meeting. After the meeting he makes another deal, "Call me if you want to take a drink and I'll join you," he says. The pleasantly graying doctor, with his gentle bedside manner, has over 28 years of sobriety. A fact she can't begin to wrap her brain around.

The call of the Wild Turkey is too strong, and Laura doesn't make it to sobriety at first. She has six more hellish binges then it is over.

Summer Breezes

Sitting in her office with the window open Laura enjoys the summer breeze and thinks about writing again. The opportunity to travel to Italy is past. Sean's calls, at first frantic and passionate have become less common. Perhaps he thinks she is hopeless, but she hasn't had a drink in four months. All the booze and pot have been given away or thrown out and some calla lilies now sit in a crystal vase on the barren bar.

Cloud's hot breath on her leg causes her to reach down and hug his head. "It's been a long time buddy, but I think I may be back.

"Computer, call Stuart please."

Would you like me to call Stuart McKenzie at Jones and Sons Publishing in New York?

"Yes,"
But Stuart isn't answering this time, or the last 30 calls she has made while trying to sober up. So, she texts him.

...Stuart, I think I'm sober now. It's been over 4 weeks. Call me dammit, or I swear I will find another publisher, or worse, I'll self-publish...

The phone rings almost immediately.
"That was fast."
"Ah well, you know I've been busy."
"And I've been busy sobering up."
"Let's hope so." His tone is a bit too puckish.
"Geesh, give me a freakin' break, would you?"

"You missed your deadline, what is your new plan?"

"My new plan is to finish the book then go find Sean in some wonderful place and have a vacation, if he'll still have me."

"Well, great, text me at the end of next week and give me a status report. Look, I've got to go. I wish you well, sweetheart."

Returning to the work was not as awkward as Laura had made herself believe. Getting back on the phone with Sean is another matter. She decides to do a soft inquiry by returning Judy's month-old message.

...Have some news concerning your grandfather, please call me...

"Judy, hi this is Laura Haskell. Sorry, I've had health issues, and haven't been able to get back with you until now. Hope all is well. Please call me back." She tells the recording.

I could call Sean and tell him I got my 90-day chip. Or maybe I should wait until he calls me. His last call was over two weeks ago. Perhaps he's just busy. Oh, what the hell. She texts him anyway.

...Call me when you have a chance. I forget where you are now...

The little bubble dots dance right back. *That's encouraging.*

...Hi, how are you doing?...

...Much better. I think I'm finally getting it. I got a mean sponsor and I talk to her several times a week...

...That's terrific, I'm in Oregon. I'll call you tonight...

Getting It Right

"Computer tell me the procedure in childbirth."

Hmm... I don't know that.

Great, my character Aadya is about to give birth and I don't have a clue what that entails. She Googles it and gets some answers but still wonders if she can write with authenticity.

"Guess I'm going to have to wing it on this one," Laura tells Cloud who twists his head as if to better comprehend, but she has not given him enough information to make a good judgement.

When Judy finally returns her call, Laura is down in the hotel kitchen sampling a new menu item with Chef David, who she thought was looking pretty good these days since she has sobered up.

"Hey, Judy, what's up?"

"You might want to sit down for this."

Laura looks over at David who looks a little bit pissed off she has answered her phone while he was trying to get her reaction to a tall pear, apple and fennel salad. *The taller the food the more expensive.*

Reading his disgruntlement, she tells Judy, "Yeah, can I call you back in about 20 minutes? I'm with the Chef right now."

"Sure, I'm calling about your grandfather."

Even with the temptation of the tiny mascarpone chocolate cakes awaiting her approval, Laura has a hard time putting the phone down. She does it though duti-fully.

"So, where were we?"

"The salad." Chef says tersely.

The presentation is much more casual than Chef normally does, where he sits her down at a linen cov-ered table and serves a full course meal for her to sample with various vintages and hues of wine. He is leaving for France that afternoon and wants his staff to have the okay on these two items. *Maybe he's trying to take the focus off alcoholic beverages with this fast and furious tasting. At least he consults me. I guess that's because I'd throw a fit if he didn't.* Laura is just beginning to get a picture of what her behavior had been like while she was drinking.

It's Not What You Hoped For

On her way back up to her suite Laura calls Judy. "Have you found anything?"

"Well, it's not what we had hoped for. The DNA does not match with our guy. So, it's back to the drawing board."

"How do you go about that?"

"I'll have to dig in and do more research. It's okay. Sean is adamant this DNA matching is the key to our validity."

Laura sighs, feeling a little hijacked. *Maybe I should call Michelle. Don't want to, but they say I should call my sponsor frequently if I want to stay sober.*

Laura gets off the phone with Judy and immediately dials Michelle's number. Michelle is her sponsor whom she has spoken with twice on the phone and met with in person once. She is a 28-year old fireball with a red-tinted afro. Laura has selected her to be her guide to the 12 steps and thus her sobriety not because they have anything in common other than they are both drunks, but because she finds strength in this young woman's words when she speaks in meetings.

"Watcha' been doin' girl, I thought you were going to be serious about this program?"

And there was the fireball part. I should have chosen someone older, more understanding. Someone I can relate to, not a secretary in the financial district.

Faced with Michelle's jab, Laura thinks carefully about how to present her problem. "We haven't talked in a while. I was hoping we could meet for coffee today. She could hear the stifled laughter in Michelle's voice.

"Girl, I got to work, unlike some people I know."

Are you shitting me? "I work." She mutters trying not to sound defensive.

"I get off at four, let's do this then."

"Where?"

"Can we do the Verve again? It's close for me and I've got a punch card. I'll meet you at 4:30."

"Okay." She ends the call. *How in the world is this girl going to relate to my problems with a ghosthunter boyfriend and a secret grandfather, paramour to a famous bordello owner?*

Despite her reservations she immediately starts planning her route. *I'll take the cable car over to Powell & Market then the vintage electric cars down Market to the nouveau trendy Verve Coffee Roasters.* A surprising surge of relief sweeps over her.

"Come on kiddo' she tells Cloud. "Let's get out of here for a nice walk before I leave."

Us Alcoholics

Laura stares at Michelle who has returned to the table with their two lattes

"You should have let me buy."

"You bought last time," then Michelle laughs, now realizing Laura has more money than she'll ever dream of having. "Maybe I should have," she says setting Laura's coffee down in front of her on the table.

"So, what's on your mind girl? You still thinking about steps 1, 2 and 3? Or have you graduated?"

It was sponsor humor, rabid with trite sayings, overused slogans and acronyms like, HALT, EASY DOES IT and THINK.

"Are you thinkin' about drinking again?"

Laura takes a deep gulp of air. "Of course, I'm always thinking about drinking."

"Well, you just gonna' sit there and stare atcha' coffee or are you coming straight with me?

Laura's lips turn up in a smile, while her brain still struggles with her complex situation. "Look I don't know where to begin. I have this life that's a little out of the ordinary, but I've got issues and I need some help with my... resolution if you will, of my current situation."

"Oh that, of course. Honestly, I haven't talked with you enough to know much about you. I know you come to meetings at the church on Flint street, that you some kind of writer or somethin." Michelle looks into her eyes while clutching her steaming coffee mug, "Spit it out honey, nobody gonna' be the judge of you, certainly not me."

"Okay. I am a writer, a moderately successful one. I own the Crescent Hotel on Nob Hill."

"Shhewee, you are buying from now on!"

Laura pauses, she understands Michelle is just kidding. *Maybe I need to choose my words more carefully.*

"Go on..."

Michelle might as well have commanded, 'perform' for without the power of the sauce Laura is too numb to explain the next part of her story, but she forges on.

"Well, not too many people know this but,"

"Your secrets are safe with me honey. That's what this program is all about. You won't get judgement from me and what you say to me is held in confidence. We're only as 'sick as our secrets'.

"So, go on."

Shit! She bites her lip. "Okay so I met this guy in New York at my publisher's. And I've had a mad crush on him ever since. He brought his crew to study the ghosts at the hotel, then everything kind of exploded. There's this technology I'm not supposed to talk about. It's revolutionary, and top secret, and somehow I'm caught in the middle"

"How's that?" Michelle blinks innocently.

"The other part of the story is," Laura shifts in her chair, one of those uncomfortable trendy wooden chairs reminiscent of the '70s.

"My grandmother, whom I inherited the hotel from, was a famous madam here in San Francisco, way back when." Michelle's eyes are now glued to Laura's every word. "She had a child with one of her clients—my mother. My grandmother never revealed his identity because he had asked her to keep it in confidence. She told my mother and I on her deathbed they loved each other, but he was married. So, my poor mother has never known who her father was, and that paradigm falls on me too. It's a source of doubt in one's own identity when you don't know where you came from."

Michelle shakes her head, "There's lots of people in that boat. That don't give you a pass to drink."

"I know," Laura says. That's not my conundrum."

"And…" Michelle motions her hand in a circular motion as if to say, 'spit it out honey I don't have all day.'

"Okay this is the secret part. The technology they are using, and I'll be real generic here, makes it possible for me to find out who my grandfather is."

"Well, that's great then. What's the problem?" Michelle leans back, emphasizing her statement.

"I don't know, I feel sort of like I'm being used, even though my goal is his goal, just for different reasons."

"I'm no mind reader," Michelle says. "But if I were to guess, this isn't about ghosts at all, but commitment."

Wrong! Laura wants to shout. *Why did I bring this up? She can't possibly help me with this.*

"Us alcoholics look at everything selfishly and letting someone into our lives terrifies us."

Now I remember why I chose her to be my sponsor. This girl can cut through bullshit like a Wusthof steak knife.

"I'm afraid I might drink again," Laura lets her cloying fear out of the cage almost involuntarily.

"That's all right honey," Michelle pats Laura's hand in a condescending gesture. "We all share that fear. You need to call me more often, read more literature, and go to more meetings if you don't want to slip again."

"But I don't have time."

"Sure, you do," Michelle gives her a mild sneer magically encompassing both contempt and compassion which then folds into a loving expression. "You, dear sister, can do this. If you don't believe, believe that I believe. Seriously, call me more often. If it's during work hours, you can text me."

Am I Still Sober?

Laura and Cloud have just returned from a long run at Golden Gate Park when the girl at the front desk informs Laura that she has a package.

It's from Judy, a new DNA kit. "Let's give this another try with a new sample just to make sure," writes Judy. "I have a couple new suspects in mind, but not quite sure what the plan is. I will keep your anonymity though. Don't worry."

Anonymity, that's ironic. Today the testing feels more benign and less intimidating than Laura had made it out to be at first. *They are never going to figure this out anyway.* As time goes by the whole ghost vision sessions are more like a dream than reality, only now Cloud is always signaling by pawing when he sees a ghost. This is often several times a day. Other paranormal enthusiasts have contacted Liam with interests of pursuing ghosting expeditions, but he is under strict instructions not to let them; and not to give out her contact information. The whole publicity thing is under wraps until 'Mark the Genius' has obtained all his patents and FilmFlix begins to release the series.

Laura throws her keys on the mottled black granite counter and heads for the fridge. She has a new ritual to replace her old consumptions of booze and pot. Oddly, it is the pot she misses most because it never made her feel physically bad. Her replacement is water, lots and lots of water, tangy fruit juices, and running several miles a day, weather permitting. Idleness is not her friend. The answer is to throw herself into her writing. She is excited about the direction of the book right now, and as she sits down each day; the story continues to write itself.

Cloud is ecstatic Laura is finally sobering up. *More runs, more adventures, more Cloud time. I'm not one to judge, but she was killing herself. At least that is the consensus from 'Team Crescent.' And she doesn't reek of sour whiskey sweat!*

Laura is about to sit down on the couch with her laptop and a bowl of red grapes when her computer pings with a Skype message. It's Sean.

"Hey there gorgeous. I've been missin' yoo! How are you doin'?"

Do you mean am I still sober? She smiles despite her cynicism. "I've been missing you too. Actually, I'm doing great. Haven't had a drink in four months and I just saw my sponsor yesterday."

"You look good. I guess it's been a bumpy road for you as it always is. I wanted you to know I haven't forgotten you. I've been trying to give you some space and, well, we've been really busy."

"Of course, I know."

She was about to mention the DNA kits when she decides to let him run the conversation. He was the one that called, and besides the whole mysterious grandfather topic is a little bit waterlogged for her right now.

"We're in Oregon and we're headed to Mexico City next. I had two ideas. Either I could stop by for a couple of days and see you, or better yet, maybe you could come to Mexico."

"Well, maybe we could have a few days in Cabo or Mazatlan. I'm not too crazy about Mexico City."

"I hadn't thought about that. I could squeeze in a couple of days at the beach I suppose. Our gig in Mexico City is going to be something we've never tackled before. Apparently, most of the Catholic churches were built on top of Aztec ruins. These will be the oldest ghosts we have ever tried to access."

He paused. She didn't fill in the gaps for him. "We've doubled our staff, many of them are researchers trying to identify the ghosts we're documenting. Who knew this was going to be such a problem?"

"Judy called."

"Yeah, I told her to stick with you. Even with a dozen more jobs under our belt, your grandmother and your mysterious grandfather are still the closest we've come to acquirin' empirical data."

"I need an app for tracking where you all are going and where you have been," she teases him.

"Don't laugh, the FilmFlix people are all over that."

"Really?"

"They are chomping at the bit, but the Crescent episode is still planned for the inaugural pilot."

Through the next couple of weeks Laura hears from Sean almost daily, sharing his exploits of the complicated shoot at the Aztec ruins underneath Mexico City.

...There are so many ghosts it's like a crowded train station. We have ancient Aztecs and Catholic priests everywhere...

...What we are learning about the culture of the ancient civilizations is incredible. The ramifications of our studies are earth shattering. We have to roll out carefully and not compromise our legitimacy...

Or

...Daisy is amazing, but we need to bring another dog in to give her a break. You want to send Cloud?...

...No, I do not want to send Cloud!...

...Can't wait to see you in Mazatlán next week. I need a break myself. It was smart of you to insist on going to the beach...

The Ocean Pounds

Sitting on the patio of their suite as the ocean pounds the beach, Laura feels like they are in Europe because of the lovely Colonial demeanor of the city, which is much larger than she anticipated. They are staying at the exclusive Pueblo Bonito. It is such a relief to be here with Sean for three days. They have made a pact to turn off their phones. And they have been very chill. She nibbles on some strawberries so sweet they taste like candy. She has before her an almond croissant, her favorite, and a steaming latte.

The morning sun bears down adding its sensuous touch to the languor of their satiated bodies from a vigorous night after months of separation.

It surprises her that she hasn't missed the booze while being on vacation. It has helped tremendously that Sean is in recovery too.

"So, what shall we do today?" She asks him.

"I dunno' You said you don't scuba dive."

"No, I'm sorry babe, it's not for me."

"How about going for a sail then?"

"Ooh that sounds delightful."

I'll call the concierge and see what they can arrange."

"So," she says lounging on the foredeck of the sailboat sipping a virgin Mai Tai with Sean. It is August in Mexico and the breeze is light and the sun hot as it washes back and forth, shielded rhythmically by the sails as the boat lifts and pushes through each wave. "How do you want to handle this long-distance thing, and are we a thing?"

"Of coorse, we are a thin'!" He says, exaggerating his accent knowing that it drives her wild.

"Oh, stop it!" she gives him the look and pushes on his shoulder, perhaps for the first time in her life thinking how nice it would be to have a little rum in her drink. *For the taste. Not the effect?*

"Come here little cutie," he says pulling her closer and giving her a full throttled kiss.

"Sean, I had the most amazing thought that I'd like a little rum in my drink, and it was for the taste, not the effect."

"Ooh you are lyin' to yourself. That can get tricky."

Maybe? "Well, maybe, but it has been easier to be sober here with you."

She turns and looks at him with deliberate eye contact. "So... What are we doing here?"

"Having fun?"

"That is such a man answer."

He throws up his hands. "Well, I'm a man"

"Do you want to agree on having an open relationship?"

"Why in God's name would I want that?"

"I have no plans to follow your around like a groupie."

"Not askin' you to."

"So, what if a young, hot cutie rubs up against you? You're not going to answer the call?"

"I tell you what. If one does, I'll hand her my phone and she can call you on speed dial and get your permission."

"I'm serious."

"So am I."

There is silence as Laura mulls around in her mind what to say next. She wants Sean to ask her to be faithful to him, but he is too clever for that.

I Have an Idea

Cloud leaps up on his hind legs greeting Laura. Then he methodically sniffs her luggage, her shoes and her clothes. *Sean! But no Daisy. And Ocean!*

"It's good to be home. I love you too! Big boy. Mano, mano did I have fun." She slips off her sandals and there is still a small amount of sand that slips out onto the floor. The weekend's events play back in her mind with the euphoria of a powerful drug for the rest of the evening and it is difficult to sleep despite how tired she feels.

The next day when Laura checks her email, she sees Judy's research has led her to two more likely suspects for the answer to who Laura's grandfather is. Out of the three one is deceased, and the other is in a nursing home.

Jackson Holmes was a Senator from the State of California. He had one son who was killed in a car crash. There is also a granddaughter who currently lives in Santa Fe.

Levon Holt - is 97 years old and is currently residing in a facility in Long Beach, CA. He was the police chief of San Francisco. He has two daughters and six grandchildren. So multiple opportunities for getting DNA there.

Macalister Murphy (I have ruled out temporarily, while you have mostly northern European DNA, Murphy was an Irish diplomat and there is nothing to indicate he would be related to you at this time,

although we will hold him in reserve.)
These are my best guesses at this time based on
your grandmother's diary, records and other sources. I have hired a private detective to obtain DNA
samples and I don't even want to tell you the process. Nothing illegal, but still don't want to put you
in the loop on that.

Laura closes the email. *Crap, this is taking too long.
Glad I haven't mentioned it to mother yet.* Laura is inde-
cisive today about which way to go with the book. Un-
familiar for the most part with writer's block, because in
the old days before she quit drinking, she would pour a
glass of whiskey and let the ideas flow no matter what
direction they took her. *That's not happening.* Now all she
can think about is Judy and her fruitless search. She picks
up her phone and starts texting her.

... Got your email. Why do you keep looking at
these high-ranking officials?...

It takes a few minutes but finally Judy writes back.

...using her diary as a go by. Because she selected
the father in the calculated way that she did, she is
more likely to pick someone with status...

...I disagree. She told mother and me that she was
in love with this man, that he was married and that is
the reason she wouldn't disclose who he was...

The bubbles pop and crackle, but Laura doesn't wait for Judy's reply.

...I have an idea...

The bubbles stop then restart again.

...what's that?...

...I pass by this beautiful portrait of my grand-mother almost every day in the lobby, painted by artist Charles Shelton. That's all I know about the painting except for the fact that he was a friend of hers. My grandmother wasn't a vain person, but this painting was there when I took over the hotel. Will you take a look at him and let me know what you find? Maybe you can track down some of the old "sex workers" who might know something...

...I already have. There is only one living survivor. Many of them were taken out by the AIDS epidemic. I contacted her a couple of weeks ago, but never heard back...

...try her again...

Laura lays down her phone and turns to the computer in front of her. "Computer, tell me what you know about an artist named Charles Shelton. He would have lived in San Francisco in the '50s. or '60s.

Charles Shelton was a well-known portrait artist in San Francisco (1914-1984) who painted many of

the country's political leaders of the time. His work is represented in over a half dozen museums and public buildings around the country including, the Library of Congress, the Robert F. Kennedy Dept of Justice, Crystal Bridges Museum of American Art and the Palace of the Legion of Honor.

Would you like to know more?

"Yes."

Artist Charles Shelton was born in British Honduras. His father was Victor Shelton, a British envoy who was sent to British Honduras to help stimulate the economy. There he met Gambrella Shana, a local singer/actress who left British Honduras, and, taking the young Charles with her, emigrated to San Francisco where she was promised a leading role in the musical "All That Glitters." The part never materialized, but the young Shelton began painting portraits to help support himself and his mother. The painter's reputation grew, due in part to his friendship with Madam "Sally" aka Elizabeth Schuster of the famed Bradley Mansion on Maiden Street, who introduced him to many of his clients.

Holy Shit, this is it! Their relationship is even mentioned in Wikipedia. "Siri, dial Judy"

Would you like me to dial Judy Malcolm or Judy Albrew?

"Judy Malcolm."

It takes forever for Judy to answer, but she finally does.

"Judy, I think I've found him!" Laura's breath comes in short and rapid strokes like a sump pump running out of water.

"You need to look into artist Charles Shelton. I think he's my grandfather."

...What have you found out?...

Laura texts Judy.

It's only been a day, since their conversation, and Laura is antsy to move the investigation forward. Judy doesn't reply so she texts Sean.

His picture pops up on her phone when she punches in his number. *I miss him.*

I miss him? Memories of their time in Mexico cascade across her consciousness with dopamine pleasure.

...Hey trying to connect with Judy, is she there with you?...

...No, she's with the crew right now, I'm worn out. Taking a nap...

...You're not getting sick are you?...

...No, just tired. You know the insane hours we keep...

...I miss you...

The words leave her fingertips and Laura can hardly believe what she has done. Is she actually starting to feel again? Her sponsor Michelle said this might happen.

The next thing she knows she is surprised by the ringing of her phone. It is Sean. "Hey, I'm glad you called. Did Judy tell you I think I've figured out who my grandfather is?"

"Yes, let's hope so. If this is the real deal we will return to San Francisco and shoot some more. Then we'll be able to let this genie out of the bottle. It's about time Mark the Magician gets his Nobel Prize."

"What about you? This is your life's work don't you get a prize?"

Sean laughs and throws on his heavy accent. "Gurl yoo are ma prize. Besides I'm gettin' filthy rich."

Later that night Judy calls and shares with Laura there are two living descendants of Charles Shelton, two sons from his marriage. "I'd prefer to go the direct route," she tells Judy. I would like to be honest about why we want to find out instead of all this sneaking around. Please let Sean know of my wishes"

But Judy persists. "It's an easy process for the Private Investigator to legally get a DNA sample without their knowledge. Don't you watch TV?

"Let me know the minute you know something." Laura says, trying to conceal her frustration.

"I've got to tell you, this might explain some of your DNA which traced back to some ancient bloodlines in Central America."

"What do you mean?"

"Well, if our hunch is right, your great grandmother was a native of the British Honduras, which is now Belize and those bloodlines go back to the Incans."

Laura hangs up the phone. She tries to go back to reading. It is no use. *Booze! Now wouldn't that be freakin' dandy? if I could drink myself to sleep?*

It is ten o'clock and she doesn't like to run in the dark, but the gym on the fifth floor doesn't seem nearly as beneficial as a good run. Besides no one would approach her with Cloud by her side.

"Wake up Cloud, we're going for a run."

It's as You Suspected

A week later Laura hears back from Judy.

...It's as you suspected, Charles Shelton is your grandfather. We got two sources of DNA and are confident. We don't have an image of Charles Shelton though...

...I would think having an image of my grandmother would be enough...

...As to that point we need to get your mother to identify her or anyone else who would be a viable witness. Sean still wants images of your grandfather. We are scheduling a return appearance at the Crescent. The scheduling people will get in touch with you...

...k...

Laura punches in the numbers to call her mother.

"Hello dear, how are you?" Laura resists the pulse of shame her mother's poised aristocratic voice causes her. Picturing her in her pricy Christian Louboutin heels, a pinstriped Saint Lauren pantsuit and tasteful pearls, Laura forges on.

"I'm good. I have something, well several things to share with you and it is all mind boggling. Are you sitting down?"

"I am now, what's up?"

"I didn't want to tell you about this until I was further along, but I've had almost 4 months of continuous sobriety."

"Oh Laura, that's wonderful," *Dead Air. Not without good cause. She is clearly not riding this cart without a pony.*

"I think it's really going to happen for me. I had become such a mess." *More silence.*

"Well, I know you are skeptical. I understand."

"How's Cloud doing?" *Change of subject. She's absolutely not buying it.*

"Oh, he's right here with me, as always."

"Mom, do you think you could come out for a visit?" *The silence is much shorter this time. She's trying to conceal her shock.*

"What's the matter Laura? Are you all right?"

"I'm fine. You know that man I told you I was seeing?"

"The ghost hunter?"

"Yes."

"You're not getting married, are you?"

"No!"

"Then what is it?"

"Well, I know it must be painful for you to come here and stay at the hotel. I know you have a lot of resentment toward Nanu, but I have some really big news."

"What is it dear?"

"Through the research they've been doing for the FilmFlix series we have identified your father."

Deep cave silence.

"We have DNA proof."

"What?"

"I figured it out actually. They used my DNA to match it. It's artist Charles Shelton."

"Oh my God! Are you sure?

"He's the man that painted her portrait that hangs in the lobby."

"I know. She loved that painting." More stillness pours from her mother's end of the conversation like sticky tar on a cold day. "There's another portrait you don't know about Laura."

"What are you talking about?"

"Well, I thought it was distasteful, but I couldn't bring myself to destroy it. It's pretty lewd."

"It's another painting by Charles Shelton...which makes complete sense now."

"How so?"

"Your grandmother, my mother," her mother's words are crisply bitter. "is posing in a very seductive costume laying prostrate on a Victorian day bed. The artist painted himself into the picture."

"What?"

"You can't see his face or anything, you see the back of his head and part of his body sitting in a chair across from her. The quality is excellent, if not a bit on the vulgar side."

"Where is the painting?"

"Somewhere in our attic. I haven't come across it in years."

"Mother," Laura lowers her voice in the most authoritarian tone she can muster. "You need to find that painting and send me a picture of it. Get it out of that hot attic, it could be immensely valuable."

Cloud starts barking and won't stop. "Hush!" she tells him but it's no use. "Mother I'm going to have to go, someone must be at the door. Listen, I need you to come out here when the crew gets here in a few weeks. I'll let you know when. You have to come and bring the painting."

She shuts the phone off and goes to the door. There is no one there. Cloud shoots past her and runs down the hallway, growling as he goes. It takes her a few minutes to get his attention. "Bad dog!" *I can't believe his behavior! I haven't had to scold him like that since he was a puppy.* Cloud trots back and whines and paws her. His ruff is still sticking straight up. *I saw him Laura! It's so frustrating she does not see! That's the guy she is talking about, her grandfather. He's here in the hotel.*

The Mother Lode

"Come on Cloud we're going back up into the attic. There's got to be something in that room we can find about Charles Shelton."

Cloud pulls himself up off the couch and shakes. *Okay then let's get on it. I've seen him here in the hotel, but you don't seem to get it.*

Laura hasn't been in the attic room since that night when the whole crew was there filming her grandmother. The cobwebs have been disturbed by the invasion of the film crew and the trunk and books have been moved over to a different corner of the room. It is late afternoon, and the light is still shining through the window. Laura has brought a steaming cup of chai tea with her. *I know I've been through that trunk before but maybe I will find something today anyway.* Judy had returned the diary and little black book months ago and Laura has been over those items multiple times to no avail. *If there is anything... anything at all, it's got to be here in this room.* She turns on the overhead light although it provides little illumination. Setting her tea down on the windowsill she decides to pull the trunk over to the window to take advantage of the natural light. It's heavy. *Shit! Broke a nail.* She runs her adjacent finger over the rough terrain of her snaggled nail. It is mostly gone.

Cloud whines to encourage Laura and she gives him a frustrated look. "Well, you're not much help." She grabs the handle again and pulls harder. The dry, aged leather gives way causing her to lose her balance. She lands on her butt on the dusty floor. "Damnit!"

Unable to totally give up cussing per the suggestion of her AA sponsor, Michelle, who is now her self-proclaimed moral compass. Laura has toned it down a bit. She stands up and brushes off her jeans that are now caked in millions of dead dust mites. She picks up her mug and takes another sip of the pungent tea. Setting it back down, she decides to push the *damn thing.* She has to crouch down low to get the leverage she needs when she feels something release. *Well I'll be damned!* It is a secret compartment she has found, and it is the mother lode.

Cloud begins to paw nervously pointing to Nanu who is standing nearby laughing. She appears in a 1940's style chemise and is holding a long cigarette holder. Clouds motions are not lost on Laura, but she doesn't understand them. She whips out her cell phone and videos him in action then texts it to Sean.

As she unloads the tray in the false bottom of the trunk there are dozens of photos to go through. There are too many to carry in her hands, so she picks up the whole false bottom compartment and carries it over to the window. Many of the photos are black and white, some are faded color. There are a few really creepy ones of men in compromising positions that might have been used as protective blackmail. *Ooh, what a sordid business.*

Then Laura comes across what she is looking for. There are several photos of Nanu with a man, possibly her grandfather. One of them is on the beach. They are both in '60s vintage bathing suits and her grandmother looks stunning. The man she is standing with has his arm wrapped around her and is playfully kissing her forehead.

He is obviously smitten. Young Elizabeth stares straight at the camera. There is a palm tree in the background and a surfboard leaning up against it. The man has on tightly fitting swimming trunks which reach down to his muscular middle thighs and are tied with a drawstring. He's well-built with an admirably tanned, bare chest. He stands a few inches taller than her grandmother. It's hard to tell from the photo, but he looks fair-haired and that would make sense with the minimal hair on his body. *Looks like an acceptable grandfather. Half British and half ancient Incan, this was plausible.*

Elizabeth, with her shoulder length dark curls, is wearing an elegant two-piece suit with wide shoulder straps lifting up her generous bosom in the cupid's kiss formation of the day. The bottom half of the white cotton suit adorned with pineapples has generous lines, like what they would call boy cut today, only not fitted. *Nothing risqué at all about this photo.* Nanu's lipstick is heavy, the only element to her makeup that looks contrived. *There are those beautiful eyebrows. I would kill for them. She was a natural beauty. She did not have to sell her body the way she did. Maybe she didn't, maybe she was just a businesswoman with ruthless morals.* It was possible this wasn't Charles Shelton but, then Laura flips it over, and in the watery signature of an old-fashioned fountain pen, Laura sees "me and Charles – Hawaiian getaway."

The next picture she finds is of Elizabeth and Charles in front of a Christmas tree. Nanu is dressed in an exquisite deep red velvet dress with a large circular skirt of the times. The low scoop of the neckline is proper but still quite visible are the voluptuous mounds of Elizabeth's bosom and around her neck is a hefty load of diamonds packaged in what is probably platinum *because who would mount those rocks in anything else, right?* Her grandmother is holding a baby as stiffly as anyone would wearing those long evening gloves. *Most people don't wear that kind of 'ice' when they are posing for a family Christmas portrait.* On the back it simply says, 'we celebrate Christmas – 1954.' And so, it goes as Laura pores through the dark secrets of her family history. *If mother were here, she might have more answers to this puzzle.*

Laura's phone buzzes, it is Sean texting her back.

...I believe from your video that Nanu is there in the room with you...

...try asking her for a sign...

Laura looks up and around the room. Her body is tingling with a thousand hair follicles abuzz. "Nanu, if you are here in the room, can you give me a sign?

Suddenly the time defiled roller shade goes down and with it, darkness envelopes the room. As rapidly as it comes down it slaps back up to the roller, causing a blinding effect by messing with Laura's eyes.

Holy Shit! The phone rings. It is Sean. "She's here. She's here in the room with us. My God, I've never had the chills like this.

"Stay focused, Laura. You're safe. She is not a hostile spirit." The sound of his voice soothes to keep her from bolting, which every fiber in her body is telling her to do.

"Sean, I've found what I was looking for. I found a false bottom in this trunk. I've found pictures of my grandmother with Charles Shelton. I have enough here for a damn memoir!"

Two Moons of Merth

When Laura finally gets back to her desk, all she can think about is writing the story of her Grandmother. She is stalled with the "Two Moons of Merth." *I love my characters, but... c'mon Laura, this is nothing you haven't pushed through before... but I'm sober now. Arguing with myself is counterproductive.*

Laura writes:

At the feast for their return from their honeymoon, Aadya found herself seated next to her new mother-in-law who was full of inappropriate questions for the new-lyweds.

"Mother, please don't press my bride," Poma tried to intervene.

"We had a lovely time, let's just leave it at that. All is well in the bridal chamber."

But Aadya, feeling joyous and a little inebriated from the obscene selection of extravagant wines the servants kept pouring for her, whispered to Queen Mesa, "I am so in love with your son. We are so very happy."

The irony of writing about inebriation is not lost on Laura. *Maybe I can't drink, but my characters can.*

Laura's writing is interrupted by Sean's Skype call. "I wanted to hear your voice and report in." *He looks tan and vigorous. Delicious.*

"It looks like we will be back there at the end of the month."

"Oh good, I'm trying to help my mother schedule her visit so she will be here when the crew is here. I know you want to interview her." She pauses. "I want her to meet you of course, but don't want her to be here the whole time you are."

"I'm looking forward to meeting her."

"That sounds contrived."

"Maybe a little."

"Why don't you go ahead and come now. You've got that crew turned into a well-oiled machine. We could have a couple of weeks together before they get here."

She can see it in his face as he struggles with his decision to desert his damn ghosts.

"I'll tell you what, I will precede my crew by one week, and we can have some time together."

Laura feels a trickle of joyous satisfaction pushing itself up through the crust of her repetitive days of writing, writing and more writing.

"Okay, that would be wonderful!"

Mother, God Love Her

"So, you're coming out here next Tuesday?"

"Yes, does that work for you?" Her mother's benign question inadvertently sets off triggers so ingrained they probably formed in utero.

"You need to be here when the crew is. You need to see for yourself what is going on here. And they want to interview you. I'm not sure when that will be yet. Sean is coming a week prior to that. I want you to meet him, but he's only going to be here for a week."

"Laura, I get it. I'm going to have to ship that damn painting anyway. It's too large to be a 'carry on.' I'm sorry."

"No, that's okay."

"I'll have to have it crated, not sure if UPS will ship it, but they probably will."

"Let's have you come out a little later in the month. I'll let you know when. You say you haven't purchased the ticket yet?"

"No, I was waiting to make sure it was a good time for you. I'm looking forward to meeting your fellow though."

Fellow? Really?

"His name is Sean. I think you'll like him." *Don't let yourself get sucked into acting like a spoiled teenager with her.*

"If you're happy then I'm happy. But you're not interested in marriage?"

"Hell no!"

"Well, I hate to say it, but I guess I'm never going to have grandchildren."

Laura is overtaken by the anger surging through her body. "You're going to go there? I sobered up. Can't we at least focus on that?"

"Yes, of course dear."

"I guess if you wanted grandchildren you should have had more kids." *And there it was a complete reversion to adolescence.* "It's ironic isn't it? Nanu went to such great lengths to have you to leave behind a legacy, and the torch stops with me." *Clearly, she couldn't stop herself.*

"You're not too old."

"Forget it mother, it's never going to happen. You were focused on your career and didn't want a pack of kids. I should have the same rights."

"You're right. I had no mother role model and I was a career woman myself...at least my career was legitimate."

How could a powerhouse corporate attorney be such a whiney baby?

"I need to go, I'm getting another call," Laura lies.

"Sure. Let me know when you want me to come out. Love you honey."

"Love you too."

Laura didn't set her phone down, instead immediately began texting Michelle.

...Help I just got off the phone with my mother. Can u talk?...

...Not right now the partners have me scrambling. CU at the meeting tonight?...

Laura looks at the time. She could still make the 5:00 meeting if she scrambles.

...yes, CU then...

A Work of Art

Laura and Cloud are out running when the painting arrives. The large wooden crate delivered to the front desk is heavy and made of composite plywood so fresh it still has that wood smell to it. It stands nearly six feet tall.

"I didn't know what to do with it," the girl at the front desk tells her.

"No, problem, it looks like I'm going to need some help taking it out of this crate. Those screws will take a power drill. Ouch!" Laura gets a splinter when she runs her hand across it. She gathers her mail from the antique postal cubby behind the desk while Cloud sniffs the large box and learns immediately, from the cacophony of odors, it has traveled great distances. When he looks up there is Nanu's grinning image peeking at him from behind the crate. Knowing that it's useless, he can't resist the urge to nudge Laura with his cold nose to tell her of Nanu's presence. It's inevitable, no recognition. *Dammit, I wish she could see Nanu like I can.* They walk to the elevator and Nanu gets in too. *She clearly wants to be close to her Laura.*

It takes about a half an hour for Tim to show up with the crate on a dolly and his power tools. He struggles to fit the awkward parcel through the door, and down the two steps into the living room.

"Over there," Laura points toward the fireplace. He begins to loosen the panels of the box with the drill he has pulled from his tool belt. Cloud sees Nanu sitting in the corner waiting patiently for the look on Laura's face.

When Tim pulls off the large front panel. There is a heavy ornate, gilt frame encasing the portrait. Laura steps back to take it in "Wow, it looks like an Edgar Degas painting!" Pride warms her like a hot beach breeze. *What a wonderful artist my grandfather was.*

Nanu's apparition gets up and hugs Laura, but all she feels are prickly chills wreaking havoc the length of her forearm. "It's amazing!" she says more to herself than Tim or Cloud. Tim, a student at the San Francisco Art Institute, pulls back to examine the painting himself.

"It's a little crisper than a Degas, and the color is bolder, but man how beautiful it truly is," he says.

Laura takes a second look at this young man working for her and is surprised by his knowledge of art. "I'd like to hang it over the fireplace. We'll have to get that other piece down first."

"Sure," he tells her then pauses to study the painting to be removed more closely. "That looks an awful lot like a Robert Motherwell."

"That's because it is," she chuckles at her own good fortune to own the piece, purchased in Boston when she lived there. *Not everything about my marriage to John was a loss. We shared art in common.*

"We'll find somewhere else to place it, don't worry."

Once they get the portrait hung, Laura studies the image.

Her famous grandmother known as 'Sally' in her professional days, is draped languorously over an intricately carved Victorian lounge settee with sensuous lines that mimic 'Sally's' own voluptuous curves. The image of the velvet upholstery looks soft enough to touch. It is the sil-

131

houette of the artist studying his model that is particularly haunting. The overall seductive nature of the painting brings to life both lust and love in a problematic juxtaposition. While she has never seen anything quite like this erotica in a major museum, the skill and power of the image certainly make it museum worthy and it will now be the centerpiece of her living room.

"I think you are right. The lines are crisper than a Degas, but the painting is idiomatic of that period."

"Look at her costume," Tim says. "The detail is extraordinary.

"Yes, it's extraordinary." The minute details of Nanu's attire, with its baubles and baby's breath lace, punctuate her curves... *I have her lips and eyes.*

Like Birds at a Feeder

When Sean arrives a week later all routine gets tossed. Cloud never knows when they are going to take him for a run or feed him. *At least I've gotten him trained to feed me in the morning. All I have to do is stomp around on Sean's side of the bed until he gets up. The last couple of days he's even pulled on his sweats and taken me downstairs to pee. Next on the agenda is to go ahead and get him to take me for a run. I may have to do a little more sucking up.*

Laura is always laughing when he is around and mellow. He's looking more and more like a keeper for our pack.

With his belly full, Cloud curls up on the window seat in the deep shelter of pillows which he stomps until they are exactly right and lies down in the growing warmth of the morning sun.

He pricks his ears as he hears the two of them talking in the bedroom and quite frankly can't completely understand what the topic is about.

"I'm thirty-eight."

"So?"

"You're almost 50."

"So?"

"You have children."

"They're almost grown and live in another country."

"I only have five months of sobriety."

"Well, now you've got me there." Sean says to her.

Cloud decides to check in with them. Jumping off the window seat he trots into the bedroom where he feels the tension building between the two of them like prickly static before a rain.

"I'm sorry I can't go there. Let's just keep having fun and not worry about the future. My mother will be here tomorrow and don't even think of giving her ideas."

Laura gives Sean her most stern look of disapproval. *That's the face she makes at me when I do something really naughty like when I pull something out of the trash when she isn't looking.*

"Well, to let you know, I will be soon be set for life, and while I'm not ready to retire, I am ready to slow down." Sean says pulling on his shirt.

"You are?"

"Hell yes, it's been a very excitin', but strenuous year for me."

"Come on," he gently slaps her on her leg. "Let's go to the attic and see if we can't get 'ole' 'Sally' to come out. I brought an AI unit with me and I've been dying to try the head set on Cloud.

Okay then let's go! Cloud heads for the door and starts circling manically to let them know he is on board.

"Look at what you've done. You're going to turn my dog into a ghost dog."

"Lucky dog." Sean tells her throwing his equipment knapsack over his shoulder and escorting the two of them out to the elevator."

Cloud is more than accepting of his role in ghost hunting as he bows his head for Sean to slip on the head-set.

"Well, there she is!"

"Oh my God!"

Nanu is sitting in the rocker in the attic with a calico cat in her lap.

"We've found with this equipment; we don't have to work in the middle of the night like we used to."

"Why is that?"

"I dunno'. I suspect it's because we have such powerful connection with them now and we don't have to avoid interference as much. The apparitions are sensitive to the environment though. We still have to be gentle with them. They are like birds at a feeder, you have to respect them, or they'll flutter off. They don't like loud noises or being startled."

Driving a Classic

"Oh my God this car is amazin'!" Sean says as he pulls the tarp off the classic beauty.

"Told you," Laura gives him a playful pat.

"And this came with the hotel?"

"Yes, it was my grandmother's, of course."

"And you say it's a '56 Daimler coupe?" He asks running his hand over the round haunches of the creamy white vehicle.

"Yes."

"Well, you've got to marry me now."

"Oh, stop. I knew you would wet your britches over this, but I didn't think it would be this bad."

"Does it run? We could take it to pick up your mother at the airport tomorrow."

"Does it run? Of course, it runs," *He knows so little about me.* "Well if you knew me at all, you'd know I keep everything in top shape."

Sean gives her a funny look. *Maybe I'm taking this too personally.*

"I don't drive it often. Mostly we park it in front of the hotel on occasion to create a little buzz. And I was just going to have an Uber pick mother up."

"You're kidding right? When we could drive this? That doesn't sound friendly. I want to make a good impression with her."

"Oh, you're going to do that all right."

"How about a little test drive? So, I can practice handling her in traffic," Sean says opening the car door and signaling for Laura to get in. "D'jou bring the keys?"

"Yes, I figured you'd want to take her for a drive."

Cloud barks once. *Wha' the f*! Don't forget I'm here.*

"Oh righto, we'll not be leaving you behin'. Get in big boy." The excitement has caused Sean to lapse into a heavier brogue than usual. He opens the back-seat door for Cloud who pounces onto the seat like it is prey.

Sally's apparition takes her place beside Cloud in the back seat. They make quite the spectacle driving down the streets of San Francisco with the top down. Most only see the big white dog in the back seat, but for a select few there is a double take as they spot a woman dressed like a flapper girl, grinning from ear to ear with her hand atop the big dog's head.

This is how they greet Emily the next day at the pick-up curb. Pleasantries are exchanged. And Laura puts her mother in the front seat to shield her from the wind.

Cloud loves the way the cold Pacific air tickles his nostrils as they speed away from the transportation hub where people with all kinds of exotic scents disembark. He has been here several times before and each time it is a sensory overload he welcomes. He notices people staring and he assumes he is the object of their desire. *Or it might be this dope car. Who knows?*

Close Encounter

"So, take me right to the attic," Emily says almost the minute they hit the hotel.

"Don't you want to freshen up a little, relax and get something to eat? You've just flown across the country for heaven's sake."

"No, I'm good. Well, on second thought I have been traveling all night on the 'red eye' maybe that is a good idea."

"Would you like to take a nap?"

"No, I need to power through. If I go to sleep now, I'll get my system all messed up on top of the 3-hour difference in time."

"I was wondering why you took that flight. It's not like you can't afford a daytime flight."

"Laura, I had to. You wanted me at a certain day. By the time I booked my ticket that's all that was left."

There it was, the searing guilt she could deliver without any premeditation. "I'm having your luggage taken up to the suite next to mine. So, you'll be right down the hall from me."

As they climb to the eighth floor on the elevator, Cloud sees 'Sally' has joined them and clearly is happy to have her daughter and granddaughter together in one place. Cloud moves past Laura to get near Emily. *She's been talking about her mother. This has got to be her. I can tell by her scent they are family.*

When the elevator stops it lurches a little more than usual and everybody wavers.

"Whoa, Nellie!" Sean remarks, causing Laura to giggle.

"I guess we ought to have this deathtrap looked at," she says.

"So, your suite is down the hall." Laura points and hands the key to her mother.

"Woof." *I'll show her.* Cloud wags his tail and the two of them head for the other half of the penthouse down the hall. Emily turns around and gives Laura and Sean a perplexed look. She has never met Cloud before, and his gracious hospitality surprises her.

As they enter Emily's suite, Cloud sees Charles Shelton and "Sally" sitting on the couch waiting for Emily. The two apparitions grin at each other and hold hands. Cloud lies down patiently waiting for Emily to head out.

"Okay, Cloud are you ready? I know I am. Ready to meet my father." She looks in the antique mirror by the door and tugs at the collar of her blouse.

"Woof!" *If only you knew he was sitting right here, right now. Of course, the only way they can see the ghosts is if I wear that annoying headset.*

"We'll head up to the attic then if you're ready," says Laura when Cloud and Emily come to the door.

"I'm actually a little nervous. What if they don't show?" Emily tells her daughter.

Oh, they're gonna show honey, they are right here with us. Wait. Maybe I can get Sean to put the headset on me here and we won't have to go to the attic. Cloud goes over to Sean's backpack with the gear in it and paws at it.

"Look Laura, what Cloud is doing,"

"Woof" loud and stern comes out of Cloud. *These poor dumb shits don't know Charles and Sally are right here.*

Sean acts like he is going to pick up the backpack thwarting Cloud's plan, so he lays down on the pack defiantly.

"What are you trying to tell me chum?"

Cloud then noses the pack and barks once more.

On a hunch Sean opens the pack and pulls out his gear. "Let's see what we can right here. Cloud seems to have a plan." He pulls at the sleek Mac and plugs in the headset, while sitting down on the couch. Charles who is already sitting there pops up out of Sean's way. "Come here boy." Sean says to Cloud who lowers his head in dutiful submission so Sean can put on his headset. The computer comes alive and there in Laura's living room is the couple in question.

"Oh my God!" Emily grabs Laura's arm with the grip of the astonished, and works to wrap her brain around what she is seeing.

"I know isn't it amazing? This is the first time we have ever seen him. He's here because of you."

"Can we talk to them?" Emily looks at Sean.

"Well you can try, but their communication with us is never direct. We can't hear them if that is your expectation."

"Mother, can you see or hear us?" Asks Emily who obviously hasn't listened to a word Sean has said. Sean looks at Laura and smiles benevolently.

Softly Sean directs her with his hand motion to use her phone to video the encounter.

"Sally's" image looks at Charles lovingly and picks up his hand to hold it." Chills creep across Laura's arms and she looks at her mother through the lens of the phone to see how wildly affected she is by this display.

I'm the dog! Cloud praises himself without a shred of humility. *Without me they couldn't see any of this.*

"Mother, all these years you kept this secret. You should have told me!" Emily all but stamps her foot at the image of her dead mother in the room.

"Sally's facial expression shows a bit of contempt which quickly washes away. "Did you see that?" Laura asks Sean. "It's almost as if she is experiencing emotions."

"I wouldn't write too much into what you see as that. These images are not living people. And we shouldn't project our thoughts onto them. We must stay as detached and scientific as we can."

"You say that, but this is our family we are seeing." Emily says uncharacteristically jittery. Sean looks at her briefly then returns his focus to his computer. Laura is filming her mother's reaction and the images on the computer screen do not transfer well to the video. Mostly they look like blurry blobs. This goes on for another twenty minutes with Emily reduced to an emotional wreck as she tries to engage with the vision of her mother and father. Then all of a sudden "Sally" blows them a kiss and they both disappear like they have been sucked out of the room.

"It feels like she's protecting you from something." Sean murmurs. "Most of our sessions are with strangers. We've found when family are involved, the sighting will only last around 30 minutes at a time. We've kicked around some ideas, but we don't have a clue why that is."

Emily sits down on the couch. "I hate to ask this darling," she looks at Laura apologetically. "Do you have some bourbon stashed somewhere? I sure could use a drink." Laura and Sean both grin at each other.

"I don't keep any here anymore, but I can have someone send something up from the bar." She looks at her phone and it is almost time for lunch. "I'll have some lunch sent up for us."

"Oh, that would be nice. Order me a Manhattan please." Laura who had never known her mother to be much of a drinker didn't mind this request so early in the day. *This is a big deal for her and if that's what she wants, I'm okay with that. I'm the one that doesn't need to drink.*

"Okay, I'd like to call your father now. Should I put him on speaker phone?"

"Sure," Laura says looking at Sean. "Why don't you Facetime on my tablet and he can meet Sean.

"We can use this computer," Sean offers. "What's the number?"

"703-555-2207"

"Hey ladies!" Vincent Martin is one of those men who wears bow ties and pulls it off. He wears his curly, graying hair shorter now than he once did. "I wish I could have joined you, Laura, but they've got me teaching a few classes now at Georgetown."

"I heard. Congratulations."

"You won't believe what just happened, Vince," Emily interrupts. Her voice is uneven and libretto from the adrenaline of her experience. "We saw them. We saw my mother and Charles Shelton, my father!"

"My goodness, this is revolutionary."

"Sean is here, Dad," Laura pulls him into the camera range.

"Pleasure to meet you, sir." Sean's greeting is formal, but no one corrects him.

"So, you're the man my daughter is in love with?" Laura rolls her eyes, but there is no proper response other than yes, and this is way beyond her comfort zone.

"Yes, I am." Says Sean without skipping a beat. "I'm trying to talk her into marrying me, but so far she keeps turning me down."

Vincent laughs, "Well good luck with that."

That night Sean and Laura are lying in bed. They have eaten an early dinner and sent her Mom to bed to catch up on her sleep. Tomorrow will be a busy day with the film crew interviewing Emily.

"So, what do you think about Scotland? Sean asks her.

"I don't know," she shrugs. "I've always heard it's beautiful, but I've never been there."

"I want to get my son Michael involved in the business, and I was thinking of spendin' a little time there this summer. Lord knows there's plenty of ghosts there to study."

"Lord knows," she parrots him twisting her fingers inside of his.

"So, if I got us a little bungalow somewhere would you spend a couple of weeks with me?"

"Oh my God, that's terribly risky!'

Looking at her with total surprise he says nothing

"You want to take this perfectly wonderful long-distance relationship and spend weeks together?"

"Yes," he says seriously, ignoring her frivolous tone. "Call me an old fool, but yes I do."

Laura rolls over onto her stomach so she can see his face. *Can I do this? Can I actually be in love?*

"I guess I'm willing to suffer through a couple of weeks in Scotland then. Do they have AA there?" she asks knowing they do, of course.

He laughs throwing his head back. "Do they have AA there? Why they've got so many drunks in Scotland there's an AA meetin' on every corner."

Three Rings of Circus

When the film crew arrives the following day, it's clear the energy has bumped up several notches since they were at the Crescent last because they are now shooting segments for FilmFlix. And the Crescent is still slated to be the opening show.

"I can't believe what a circus this has become," Laura says to Sean as she watches a tour bus filled with people unload their cargo. A big box truck crammed with equipment has been added to the entourage. The number of people involved has grown exponentially. They tend to be rather young and energetic, although a few are gray haired and move more slowly as they traipse up the massive marble stairs to the lobby. "We have one whole floor, one whole floor dedicated to housing the crew alone."

Standing on the hotel steps with a cup of coffee in his hand, Sean has a mixture of pride and grim determination engraved into his expression. He gives her the humble shrug she has come to know as the 'what me worry?' stance.

"You can see why I'm ready to take a back seat. We've grown. That's spelled g-r-o-a-n."

It's one of Sean's corny puns. *I guess I'm in for a life of banal humor. It's not getting any better even when I don't react.*

"Mother is excited to do her interview." They're filming that this afternoon because she's leaving the day after tomorrow and they want to be sure they have enough footage of her.

145

"That's where we are headed first, to 'Sally's attic,'" Sean tells her. "Let's go grab a bite to eat before we head up there. I can't get enough of those blueberry pancakes," he says as he pokes out his stomach and pats it.

Before the afternoon is out the whole crew is referring to Emily as 'mom.' The interview has some charming parts, but time and again, because Emily's legal brain is arguing with her emotional side, she interrupts and says "Let's do that over. I don't like how I said that." While Charles Shelton's wife was dead, his two sons, one a successful artist in Maui and the other an aging actor with no large credits to his name, have opted for a rather robust settlement in order for FilmFlix to air this personal information about their father. Emily is careful not to say anything that might be offensive to them or their children. They were, after all, her half-brothers. They both had been rather cavalier about it, and their families, not ever having known their grandpa', weren't opposed to taking a bunch of money for a semi-scandalous heritage. And being on FilmFlix, of course. It seemed that just one generation removed, it wasn't such a big deal.

"I can't tell you how much it means to me to finally find out who my father is. This was a terrible secret for my mother to keep from me," Emily works to seduce the camera with her sad story. "I didn't actually know my mother well, until her later years. I was raised mostly by my aunt and uncle."

A makeup artist has been hired locally to ready her for the camera and she looks stunning with her white sa-

teen hairdo curling around her lower ears with professional permanence no recalcitrant breeze is going to ruf-
fle. After several hours of being interviewed Emily thinks
she has covered everything.

After the first filming, the action moves to Laura's
suite where she and Emily sit in front of Laura's fireplace
with the provocative painting of Nanu in the background
while the interviewer asks them more questions. Cloud
and Daisy are sitting with them at their feet.

"So, tell us about this painting above you, Laura."

"Sure, it was in my mother's attic for decades. I didn't
even know about it until recently. As you can imagine.
My mother has a lot to reconcile about her past. And that
is certainly understandable."

"Did you know you grandmother? Was she in your
life at all?"

"No, I didn't get to know her until I graduated from
college. She took me to Europe for a graduation present
and that's when we became close. She deeded the hotel
over to me about ten years later. I lived in Boston and she
lived here at the Crescent until she died. We wrote letters
and talked on the phone during that time. I was in an…
ill-suited marriage, and she counseled me at times. I was
just beginning to write."

"What was your grandmother like?"

Laura had thought through what she might say when
asked this sort of question. "As you might suspect she was
adventurous and a lot of fun. In her later years she was
repentant of the kind of life she had led." *Breathe. Just be
honest, this can all be edited.*

"In what ways was she repentant?" he asks.

"Well, she bought this hotel, and went legit. She helped many of the women that had worked for her to get out of the business by helping them financially with their education or housing needs.

"I would like to think…"

"Yes, go on."

"I would like to think she did more good than harm in her life. I think, while she was not the kind of mother one would hope for, she loved her child dearly and provided for her." Laura looks over at her mother who is visibly impacted by Laura's statement.

"Emily what do you think of Laura's assessment of your mother?" Emily laughs as if someone has asked her to walk on hot coals. Then pulls herself together, sitting up a little straighter. "Grandchildren have a different relationship with their grandparents than children do. Or so I'm told by my friends." She gives Laura a punitive glare and laughs.

Even on camera she pushes…

"And why do you think your grandmother haunts the Crescent, Laura?"

"That's what everybody here is trying to find out." Across the room Sean smiles at her, connecting with her in a way that makes her weaker not stronger, in the same way bloodletting was supposed to cure the sick before healers figured out it was lethal. *I can't wait for this interview to be over!*

"Can we pause a minute?" Laura blurts out.

"Sure," the interviewer says giving the signal to the film crew.

Laura squeezes out of her seated position and goes over to Sean wiping her shiny forehead, with the back of her sleeve. Her silk blouse is not absorbent, adding to her anxiety. Someone rushes to her side with a cloth and more facial powder. "What is it I should say here?"

"Just relax, be yourself. You're doing fine." He holds her arm. "Do you need to take a break?"

"No, I want to get this done. I don't really understand the physics angle you have been telling me about."

"Well, give your honest opinion. You don't have to prove anything, just leave that to me."

"I'm not sure I have an opinion."

"You're a fantasy writer for God's sake. Make something up."

"Okay," she inhales deeply three times from her diaphragm like her yoga instructor has taught her. The action registers with Laura as counter intuitive. *Inhale the belly pooches out, exhale, belly button to the ribs, but it always works.*

Laura goes back over to her position sitting beside her mother and the makeup artist does a few more tweaks, laying her golden hair gently on her shoulder just so. *I feel like an effing Barbie doll for God's sake!*

The moderator asks her if she is ready. Despite the heat and glare of the lights. She nods yes.

"And why do you think your grandmother haunts the Crescent Hotel, Laura?"

A gracious smile balloons out onto her face willfully from a place of inner resolve. "Well, given her circumstances, why wouldn't she? We don't have all the answers, but she and the other ghosts seem to be having a good time. We don't fully understand why the apparitions are here. It is only because of Sean Wilson and his vigilance we may soon know. For now, I think its fine to romanticize their presence as we always have."

"It has been an incredible experience to learn who my grandfather is, and what an interesting person and clearly gifted artist he was." She glances toward the painting above them. "He lives on brilliantly through his work. As all artists do."

The moderator chuckles and the camera switches to him. "Emily do you agree?

Emily's composed expression breaks off as she answers, "I barely knew my mother. I was mostly raised by my aunt and uncle." Emily shrugs, "She was full of drama in her life, why not in her afterlife?"

"Laura will you introduce the two dogs that are sitting with you?"

"Sure, this is Cloud my best friend and confidant," she snuggles his neck in her arm. "And this is the very famous Daisy, the first known ghost-seeing dog. We now know not all dogs can see ghosts, but we know these two can. They are both extraordinary."

"And were you aware that Cloud could see the ghosts before he wore the now famous headset?"

"Not exactly we have known the hotel was haunted for decades, and sometimes Cloud would act peculiarly, but before we put the head set on him it was not proven. No one knows yet why some dogs can see apparitions and others cannot. I guess it's the same with people. Some people are more paranormal sensitive than others."

"Have you ever seen a ghost?"

"I have now, but no, not before this new AI technology. It is my opinion; this discovery will lead to many more areas of science opening up for us in general."

Edits and Cuts

With all the interviews done and Emily delivered to the airport, all that was left to do was the reenactment of Laura finding the hidden cache of photographs in the trunk in the attic. Cloud is a big part of this this scene and Daisy's trainer, Kaley, works with him to fulfill his part as described by Laura. What happened in about 20 minutes takes them most of a full day to produce the re-telling for the screen.

Cloud finally succumbs to the fact there are no headsets today, only a monotonous routine of him and Laura moving around the room, repeating the same actions over and over again until the director finally says it's a wrap. *I guess they know what they are doing but man-o-mano this is boring.*

The one bright spot is Kaley, who is constantly giving him treats when he follows her commands. *I sure miss Emily. She was a great friend, always sharing her leftovers when they ate out, and sneaking me snacks under the table when they ate in. And she liked her meat rare!*

Once they have wrapped up the scene, Laura sneaks off to do a little work. Her efforts are in vain. After a day of being the center of attention and being fed treats every few minutes, Cloud becomes irritable with the usual routine where Laura spends hours glued to an illuminated computer screen. He trots over to her desk where she is typing away. He gives her leg a push until she acknowledges him. "Hey pretty dog. Are you bored?

"I'm trying to finish this section while I can. I'm this close to finishing the book." Laura squints and gives him a strange finger message with her thumb and finger. "It's kind of hard to get anything done with all this commotion going on."

C'mon I want to go see what's going on. You can work on this later. He pushes against her again. She is oblivious. Then the phone beeps.

"Oh, that's Sean," Laura tells Cloud. "He wants me to come to the office they've set up."

...I'll be down in a few minutes have to wrap something up...

...I need you for a while, they are starting the editing process and I need you to oversee a few things...

...sure...

Laura sucks in her breath and lets go of the idea that she will be able to dedicate anymore time this day to *The Two Moons of Merth.*

"I like that one," Laura points to the computer screen where the film editor is working. "That take is more like it actually happened," she says. "We also found a few more photos, did Judy give them to you?" Laura sits for hours with the film editor. It is fascinating for her to see the film version begin to evolve. Sean pops in and out several times but doesn't interfere much.

"Laura," he finally breaks into their work. "Did you say there is a movie theatre in the hotel?"

"Yes, it's small. It's like a home video theatre."

"How many does it seat?"

"I think 12, it's got leather loungers."

"Sweet. But that's not big enough for the whole crew. I guess for tonight's purposes we could use it and catch what you and Chamber have been working on all afternoon."

"Oh, we're definitely not ready for a full crew screen," Chamber looks up and tells Sean.

Laura picks up her phone. I'll call Liam and make sure no one is using the theatre. We can set up our ballroom for the crew when you are ready for that."

Marshall Crux pops his head in. He is the producer from FilmFlix. Laura had met him once briefly.

"How's it going guys?"

"Chamber, you've got three days to get us a rough cut and then it goes to corporate for a full-blown edit."

"Yeah, I know. Do you want to come see it?"

Marshall looks at this phone. "I've got a scheduled Skype meeting in about ten minutes."

"That's okay," Sean butts in. "We're having a first edit showing tonight. The hotel has a small screening room."

"Oh great," Marshall, who could barely be 35, tips his head up and smiles the boyish grin of someone happily working in the entertainment industry who is going places.

Popcorn and Beer

"Mmm, this popcorn is good." Sean tells Laura as he digs down into the bucket they are sharing.

It's almost midnight, but that's how long it takes to pull the screening together. No one seems to mind. The crew is made up mostly of young people who enjoy working all hours of the night.

"Ssh, I can't hear," she tells him.

"Ooh, one of those," he says giving her a disparaging look. "I wish they'd hurry up with those drinks. This salt is getting to me."

"Sshh...it's probably that real Coke you ordered. Who drinks real Coke anyway?"

"I do with popcorn."

"It's so odd to see myself up there on the big screen like this."

"I know. I don't think I'll ever get used to it."

"Oh, please. You love the camera and the camera loves you."

Sean tosses a kernel to Cloud who is sitting obediently on the floor next to Laura. His chops make a snapping sound as he reflexively catches the buttery morsel. "You're a movie star now Cloud, and a ghost dog too." *Just toss me more corn, dude, and be cool.*

"Here they come." Liam and a couple of waiters come in with a cooler full of beer, some sparkling waters and a variety of canned drinks. They waiters toss the drinks as people speak up about what they want. Everybody seems to love the casual and unconventional service and the spewing they have to guzzle when they open their cans.

"Geesh, I hope their aim is good, nothing like destroying one's evening by getting hit in the head with a flying Coke!"

"Relax, would you?"

Liam and the boys sit down in the aisles and join them. There is no music in this first cut, except for the beginning. It takes several hours to watch what will eventually be pared down to an episode length.

The producer gets up and says a few words to thank everyone involved and goes on about "This amazing scientific technology that has altered the canvas of the paranormal experience."

He pauses to look at Sean, "Would you like to say a few words Sean?"

"Shoor" Sean stands up and wipes the salt off his Hawaiian shirt. Laura is amazed at how slim he stays, even while eating like a horse all the time."

Everyone in the room waits for him to speak. He looks at them first, with those penetrating eyes of his and takes a deep breath. *God he's dramatic.*

"I can't thank everyone enough for their passion and collaboration on this project. We've been hitting the road hard this year, but we've come full circle with this thing. And it's almost time to have a little rest. Many of the episodes are completed and now that we have the footage for the inaugural episode we are about to step into another stage of our work." He pauses, "Listen to me. I'm starting to sound like I've been in film all my life.

"Anyway, we certainly don't have all the answers yet, but we've brought a lot of mystery out of this process by bringing our ghosts to the big screen. We couldn't have done it without Daisy and her new sidekick Cloud. He looks around for Daisy and asks where she is. "She's already gone to bed," says someone in the back of the room.

"Oh, that's a shame. Cloud you come up here and take a bow. Would you please?"

"Go on, it's okay," Laura urges Cloud by giving him a little push.

"This year has brought so many answers and opened up so many new questions."

Cloud approaches Sean and turns to face the audience sitting by his side. "We couldn't have done it without Daisy and her side kick here. Be sure and tell her next time you see her. She knows a lot of English." People laugh but they all know it to be true.

"Anyway, that's it for me. Just want to thank FilmFlix for their dedication to bringing this amazin' story to the screen."

Making a Break for It

The pleasure of the film's debut lingers in Laura's blood the next morning with the same intensity she feels when one of her books, after months and months of work, gets published. Sean clearly feels the same way and suggests they take the Daimler for a cruise. "We can take the dogs with us and find a place to let them run free."

It is Laura's idea of a dream date. The crew and Sean are packing up in a few days, then it will be all over. "I love that idea. I will get the kitchen to pack us a picnic."

"What about if we just go down to the Ferry Building at the market there and pick up a few things?"

"Well I like that idea, too, but parking the Daimler will be a nightmare."

"Then why don't we take the cable car down there and come back to get the car?"

"That sounds like a better plan."

"Can we take the dogs?" Sean asks her.

"Dogs can go on the cable car, but not into the Ferry Building, and we'll have to pay for them to ride on the cable car."

"Well, it would be a fun adventure for them, but I guess it's too much of a hassle. Daisy is too crucial to the work. I can't risk her getting lost or stolen."

"Of course not."

"Still I think it will make a nice break for her if we take her somewhere to run for a while. I'll give Kaley a head's up and see what time is best today for us to take Daisy out for a romp."

"Now you're thinking like a boss that's running a multi-million-dollar business," Laura says.

Sean gives her a chagrined look and tells his phone to call Kaley.

"She's good with that," he reports. "They won't be filmin' until late this afternoon anyway. They're waitin' on Chamber to get some more edits done this morning, so they know what to shoot tonight."

"I guess they are done with me then."

"Yes, you were fantastic. That part is wrapped up. We're down to a few fill-in shots."

"Ooh, you know what?" He spins around and snaps his fingers.

"What?" Sean has unexpectedly changed directions, but she loves seeing him mentally detaching from his work.

"We could run up to Napa Valley for the day. It's still early enough."

Laura is confused. "Napa Valley, but we can't go to the wineries. We don't drink."

He flashes her a 'silly girl' look, while she mentally catalogues the many times she has been there and how much fun it had always been.

"The Oakville Grocery. They have out-of-this-world deli food. And there are several haunted wineries up there. Chad Owens lives in St. Helena too. I'd love you to meet him. This is perfect." He gives her a little peck on the lips. She has never seen him this spontaneous.

"We can do a whole episode on the haunted wineries of Napa Valley," he says sweeping his hand across an imaginary story board. *And there it is. Work.*

"Who is Chad Owens," she asks. The name has never come up.

"He, my dear, is an apparition theorist, which is a fancy name for someone that writes about the scientific theories of why and how there are ghosts."

"Oh, I'm surprised you've never had him down to the Crescent, being so near."

Sean shrugs and she can see the wheels turning as he seeks an answer to her question.

"Well, he's a bit of a pompous ass, but he's written lots of books, most of which I've read. I dunno." Sean seems to be digging deeper into her question. "Ever since he heard about our AI program that shows the images, he's been bugging me for access. I guess I'm a little leery of letting him in too soon."

"So, you think the time is right now?"

"Let's play it by ear. Maybe I'll call him and have him meet us at one of the vineyards."

"I say we make a break for it!" He starts grabbing his backpack and looking for Cloud's leash. As they head for the garage Sean is so busy texting he can hardly walk straight.

"Oh, crap!" He stops and makes a little hop in frustration then gives up the texting and calls.

"Kaley, can you meet us in the garage with Daisy, we are pressed for time."

As they depart, it feels great to be out on the road with the wind in their hair. Cloud sits up for much of the trip, because he loves to know where he is going. Daisy lays down in the shelter of the back seat and lets the sun's warmth seep into her feathery coat. Sean turns up some classical guitar music because it's too noisy to talk, but to make up for it he looks over at Laura and smiles a lot. She is trying to keep her wide brimmed sun hat from taking flight and her blonde hair that isn't restrained flaps in the wind. Keeping the front windows up helps while they are on the freeway but once they get to the valley Sean slows down and they cruise at a more leisurely pace. *He appears relaxed, but something is bubbling inside of him.*

They get to Oakville a little after 1 p.m. and both are starving. They run in and sample the round sausages, wedges of cheese and pair them with several different types of crackers seasoned with garlic or rosemary. Sean grabs some pears, and they end up buying much more food than they can possibly eat in one sitting. Neither of them care. Laura looks wistfully at the wine and reminds herself what a bad drunk she had become. "What shall we get to drink?" she asks.

"I dunno, what about some of this ginger lemonade up there on the counter?"

"Yes, that looks good. Get me a large cup of that, and I'll pick up some of those tasty seltzer waters you like."

Their first appointment isn't until 3:30 at the Beringer wineries, giving them plenty of time to find a picnic spot and let the dogs run.

"This is idyllic." Sean says. And yet he is still texting.

"Isn't it though?" They have found a picnic table far enough away from the road to let the dogs play. A couple of hot air balloons with vivid silken panels float past so close they can hear the blast of the propane heaters.

"Let me have some more of that fennel sausage." Sean demands pleasantly. She uses his pocketknife and slices a couple more pieces. The knife is dull, and the slices are lumpy. The pears are perfectly ripe and juice slides down her chin when she bites into it. She rubs the syrupy nec- tar off her chin with the back of her hand.

Wine Wisdom

As they approach the Beringer estate, they head straight for the Rhine House, a 17-room Victorian mansion. "This is one of the most haunted places in the Valley," Sean tells Laura with surprising reverence.

They are greeted by a guide. When Sean tells him who he is and that they are to meet Owens, who will tour them the proper young man tells him. "Mr. Owens is well known around here. He will make a most excellent guide. I believe I saw him in the tasting gallery. I'll see if I can go fetch him for you."

It is like telling Sean the Pope is Catholic, but Sean gives him a polite nod.

"We will need to take the dogs in with us. They are 'seeing animals.'"

"Yes, sir, highly unusual, but we've been informed you will be bringing them."

By the time Owens shows up they have wandered around much of the house by themselves and learn that the winery was the first one in the valley, and also the first winery to promote tourism.

Daisy and Cloud have been busy marking. *Holy shit! This house is cool!* Cloud tells Daisy.

"I know, right? That old dude is one angry SOB"

Owens clumsily trips on the corner of one of the heavy oriental rugs as he enters, and it is possible he is a little snockered. "Hello there, ma' man!"

His voice is inappropriately loud and a tour guide, now leading a dozen or so people nearby looks up fondly at Owens and tells them Owens is a local expert ghost hunter.

"Perhaps you'll join us, Mr. Owens, and share some of your experiences with us?"

"Like the time old man Frederick threw a silver tray at me," he shouts jovially. "Sorry Chuck, I'm here to see this man." He grabs Sean by the shoulder. "This is the world-renowned ghost hunter Sean Wilson." A few in the crowd murmur, perhaps recognizing Sean's name. Sean visibly hangs his head slightly and looks at Laura as if to say, see I told you.

"Hey man, good to see you," Sean tells Owens good naturedly and sticks out his hand to shake.

Sean reciprocates and then looks over at the crowd as if to do damage control. "Sorry, folks we're working on a rigid schedule, please excuse us." He steers Owens toward the door to find a more private space. He discovers a nook with a round table and chairs in an overflow area of the Rhine House's tasting room.

Cloud goes up to sniff Owens' leg. *Hmm these pants haven't been washed in a while.* A rather flamboyant apparition, a woman in a tall hat with a large circular brim, pink satin ribbons, an unruly taffeta burst, and wearing a floor-length navy-blue dress, crosses the room sending a noticeable chill through the air. Both dogs begin pawing.

Sean and Laura observe the dogs signaling, but Owens is still clueless.

"Here let's sit." Sean motions to the table. He looks at the time and realizes the day is evaporating. "Excuse me a minute. I have to check in."

...Melissa you need to send someone up to St. Helena to get Daisy. And please book us a room at one of the more exclusive B&Bs up here. We are going to stay the night. And oh yes figure out dinner for me :] ...

Meanwhile Laura has introduced herself to Chad and they are talking amiably.

"I've known this guy since he first got into the business," he tells Laura. Chad has a bit of gray stubble on an aging angular jaw. He wears a worn corduroy blazer and gives off a disheveled academic aura. He seems to be aware that he is a little snockered and asks the waiter to bring him a coffee. "And bring these guys a glass of your 2014 Private Reserve Cab."

"No, thanks," Sean says "We're not having wine today."

"Oh," Chad looks disappointed. "I'm buying."

"Sorry man. I'm giving it up for Lent."

Chad looks puzzled. "But it's not Lent."

"Have you got a couple of cappuccinos?" Sean asks the waiter.

"Sure, how do you like them?"

"One wet, one dry. Make the wet one with skim if you don't have almond milk."

"So, I can't wait to hear about your cloak and dagger technology." Chad drums his fingers on the table.

"I'd like to invite you down to the city and take a look for yourself. Daisy here has revolutionized our world." Daisy lies next to Sean and he gives her a reassuring pat on the head.

"I've got to tell you I've never seen a dog in this place. Now there are two and isn't that white one a beauty?"

"This is Cloud, he's my dog," Laura says, "but he can spot ghosts too." *I love it when she brags on me.* Cloud's proud smile is not lost on Daisy who has come to know him as a wee bit vain.

"I'd like to give you a demonstration, Chad. But you have to sign a non-disclosure agreement."

"I can do that."

"Then you'd probably better get down to the city tomorrow, because we are packing up in a few days. They'll have the paperwork for you there but let me warn you."

"What?"

"Be prepared to be wowed. I'm so confident that we are enlisting a couple of brainiacs from Cal-Tech to bring Quantum Physics studies to the table."

"So, we're there?"

"You betcha', I know enough about this place we're sitting in, just from my dog's behavior, that wouldn't have been possible two years ago."

Owens takes a full calculated breath, "Well I'd at least like to put in my blog that we met today with more to come."

"Absolutely, you can go to our website, for more in-depth info and links."

"It's in my Favorites."

"So, can you at least run these guys through their paces for me?"

"Shoor, be glad too. We've gotten spoiled by the monitors, but I think I can show you a thing or two." He doesn't mention the equipment in his backpack.

"Daisy, Cloud, the house is yours begin marking."

Cloud leaps up on all floors like someone lit a fire under him and Daisy starts by sniffing the air. They run over to where they first saw the woman in the navy taffeta dress, but she is now sitting in one of the bar chairs where a male apparition with gray hair is standing and looks as if he is having a lively conversation with her. *Why aren't they putting the headsets on us?* Cloud goes over the Sean's backpack and noses it to remind him.

"No, laddie, we're not doing that right now. Just use your signals and let us know where they are."

Daisy stays in play with the couple, but Cloud, seeing someone lurking in the next room heads over there. Wanting to bark, he knows he must only use his paws, right for female left for male apparitions. *This guy looks like a worker bee.*

"This is freakin' amazing," Owens mutters softly. He pulls out a handheld decibel meter from his coat pocket and goes over to where Daisy is and pulls out an infrared thermometer. As she has been taught, Daisy lays down pointing toward the apparition if they are not on the move.

He watches his gauges intensely. Meanwhile Cloud has followed his apparition out the door and down into the vineyard. Laura touches Sean's arm to alert him that she is going to follow him.

There are other apparitions to follow out here, but Cloud sticks with his original fellow until he loses him in one of the cellars. He comes trotting back to Laura who is enjoying the warmth of the sunshine on her back and the walk

"It's kind of pointless without the computers isn't it?"

He rubs his head up against her leg. *You got that right, Laura boo!*

"Well, it's quite a little hike out here, but the grapes are beautiful." She texts Sean to let him know where they have wandered off to.

...I'm ready to get out of here. I'll sign off with Owens. Meet me at the car. I have a surprise for you...

...U know I love surprises...

It takes a good 20 minutes to get away from Chad once he sees the Daimler. He wants to know all about it, and then they have to go into more detail about her grandmother and the hotel. They are careful not to mention Laura's grandfather though, until Owens has signed an NDA.

Soaking It In

"Finally! I thought we'd never get away from him."

Laura gives Sean a peculiar look and laughs. "You crack me up. He wasn't that bad."

"Well, truthfully, I've got somethin' planned for us tonight."

"And what is that?"

"We've got reservations at the French Laundry down in Yountville and then we're goin' to stay in a swanky little cabin."

"Ooh nice. But you seem a little jittery. Today is about relaxing."

"I know," he pauses to look at her directly. "But we've got to get to the cottage so the guys can come and pick up Daisy. They're probably already there. Here take my phone, and text and see where they are."

"She says they are about 15 minutes out."

"Good, we are too."

"Now, this is the same cabin where Carole Lombard and Clark Gable once stayed," the clerk at the desk tells them when they check in.

"Nice car by the way," he says as he peeks around Sean to get a better look at it. "Where'd you get something like that?"

"I'm a collector," Sean says abruptly hoping to cut off the conversation.

"Is it too much to ask how much you paid for it?"

"Yes, it is actually." Laura and Sean smile at each other with the mutual satisfaction of a secret shared.

As they get back into the car, Kaley drives up.

"Hey boss, have you got my dog?"

Daisy hears Kaley's voice, wags her tail, and puts her paws up on the sill of the car making herself large so Kaley will see her. Cloud perks up too, looking a little disappointed as they pass Daisy off to Kaley in the parking lot.

"I've got a change of clothes for both you guys. I guess you didn't plan on staying up here when you left."

"I'm a little rusty at spontaneous." Sean looks at Laura, "but I make up for it in other ways."

"Hey, I'm grateful to get you away from work. I can handle a little glamping." Spreading the handles to the paper sack Kaley has brought, she is impressed to see her toothbrush.

They say farewell to Daisy and Kaley and head for their romantic little bungalow located on the edge of a vineyard.

It is appointed with enough luxurious accoutrements to even impress Laura, who is admittedly a hotel snob given her ties to the industry. It is comforting to see a fireplace, now lit and popping. Laura peers outside to the private courtyard where she eyes a whirlpool spa, and an ornamental fountain in the wall spilling water from the mouth of a lion into an ornate copper catch basin. A fruit and cheese tray sprinkled with nuts and dates awaits them on the table and sparkling apple cider is chilling in an ice bucket.

"You've thought of everything," Laura smiles and touches his arm lightly.

"I have, haven't I?" he beams. They both laugh knowing that it was his assistant who made the arrangements.

"Let's sit down a minute Laura. There's something I need to share with you."

Oh God, what is it now? We finally get some time away from the FilmFlix circus and he wants to talk?

"Come here boy, you need to join us too." Sean pats the red velvet sofa and Cloud leaps up on it.

"I didn't know how this was going to go down, but everything fell into place today."

Laura studies his face, wondering just where this is going?

"This is a little unconventional, but your mother insisted."

"Dear God, what?" She clutches the buttons on her shirt.

"Well, when I told her I was going to ask you to marry me, she requested that I give this to you instead of buying a ring without any meaning. I hope you are cool with it."

Sean pulls out a blue velvet box, his hands slightly trembling as he opens it.

"My God, it's gorgeous!" She is staring at a stunning emerald-cut sapphire the color of the sea at dawn, set between two brilliant canary diamonds in what looks to be a platinum setting. "That was my Grandmother's...only that's not a sapphire, is it? It's a blue diamond!"

"They are extremely rare." He says reverently.

"I know, I've heard about this ring, but never seen it. I don't think my mother ever wore it."

"She was saving it for you."

A sudden rush of emotion surges up through Laura's body as she struggles to even swallow. "Oh my God, Sean, of course I will marry you!"

"That's good. You were so star-struck by the ring I wasn't sure you noticed I was asking you to marry me." His emotions are in full display in his face though, he is trying to make light of the situation.

Laura leans over and kisses him, tasting him, salty and vulnerable. Cloud stands up on the unstable sofa cushions and pushes his way into the middle. His soft fur tickles and their physical connection is accentuated through the tactile sense of his feathery fur.

"Technically, since I did not pay for the ring other than to have it sized, I make this vow that I will be there for you in every other way you need me to be."

Laura meets his somber gaze, knowing this is not possible, but she loves the sentiment. She loves that Sean desires to say these words to her. "Well, let me try it on… how did you know my ring size?"

"I had a little help. Your mother brought it with her, and Liam let one of the girls into your suite the other day. They measured it from a ring I have seen you wear on your ring finger and gave it to me last night. I didn't know this was how the day was going to go, but here we are."

"It fits," Laura says slipping it on. "I am very impressed."

She takes another look at him and hesitates, but then goes ahead with her admission. "Truthfully, I was going to keep putting you off for a while."

"I know." Sean dips his head slightly and nods. "That's why I had to make my move before I left again."

Joy floods Laura like sunlight on water, pulsing, scintillating, effervescent. She pulls into his embrace and they sit awkwardly for a minute with Cloud not budging between them. Laura does not even feel terrified, the way she thought she would if she were ever lured into this chamber of horrors called love again. The fire pops and crackles and soon they are nibbling from the cheese tray.

"I'm going to undress you now," Sean announces. "I want to go out and enjoy the hot tub before the sun goes down."

Mmm, good idea," Laura says as she tastes a rich, buttery bite of St. Andres on a crisp, paper-thin cracker. He pours the cider into the flutes and they toast.

"To us," he says.

"To us….mmm, that's tasty."

He begins to unbutton her blouse and before they can even make it to the hot tub, they have pulled back the airy white linens on the king size bed.

"This will do," Sean proclaims.

"Yes, it will. But let's go soak awhile first."

"Deal!"

Their meal at the French Laundry is as spectacular as the hype. The table reserved for them is in the courtyard. They both order the Chef's Tasting menu which includes the restaurant's famous Oysters and Pearls. The Lobster Gallette is the favorite for both of them. Sean orders the supplemental Mac and cheese. Laura thinks she has landed in heaven when she tastes the Black Winter Truffle Fondue."

"So, when did Mac and Cheese become a gourmet item?" Sean asks. "Not that it isn't heavenly. Here you need to have a taste."

Laura leans over to reach his extended fork loaded with the delectable hand-cut macaroni.

"Mmm, that is amazing."

Her mouth is still full of the creamy pasta when Chef Thomas comes out to greet them. "Is everything to your satisfaction?" He asks in the aristocratic tone of a high-dollar chef.

"Oh my God yes, this is an amazin' meal." Sean tells him toasting him with his flute of sparkling cider.

"Laura, we've never met, but I know Liam, he called to make the reservation and told me this was a special evening for the two of you."

"Why yes, it is." Laura holds up her hand to show off her engagement ring as readily as any 23-year-old bride might have

"Ah, I see. We have created a special dessert for the two of you. Please save a little room."

"It's going to be hard," Sean says hungrily eyeing the next course that has been brought out. It is Calotte de Boef, the waiter tells them, "with Yukon Gold potato rosti, red wine braised cabbage, Cipollini onions and steak sauce." As is the custom with such tasting menus, the portions are small and great pride is taken in the artful presentation. The waiter looks a tad nervous with the chef standing there.

"This has been such a wonderful experience Chef. Thank you for your personal attention," Laura tells him.

"We will let you take your time, of course, then we have prepared one of your favorites, I am told."

"It's not chocolate souffle is it?" Laura asks.

"No," says the chef. "Funny, that's what I suggested, but Liam put the kibosh on that choice."

Laura grimaced. "I bet he did."

When the chef leaves their table. Laura takes her first bite of the beef. "And you're sure it's okay to eat food cooked in alcohol? It's so good."

"Some people won't do it, but the alcohol is cooked out, so no need to worry." Sean waves at the waiter. "We are out of herbal tea."

"Yes, sir. Right away."

Laura is amazed at how much she has eaten. And thinks about crashing in that soft bed waiting for them with the warmth of the cozy fire. She glances at the ring, then at Sean, and feels like she is a character in one of her own novels. The waiter brings them more hot water for their tea.

"I'd like a cappuccino with dessert, please."

"Black coffee for me." Sean pipes in as he wipes his last bite into the decadent sauce with his fork and pops it into his mouth.

It is not until they are settled with their coffee that the waiter brings out their dessert. It is a petite round cake for two with a light green marzipan crust and elaborately flowered in a white icing motif.

"Oh, I don't believe this! It's a princess cake. My absolute favorite. I can't believe they did this on such short notice."

Sean beams with pleasure as the evening has gone well.

They rise the next morning when someone comes to the door with their breakfast and lays it out on the courtyard table for them. Before he crashed last night, Sean filled out the menu request, even including extra link sausages and scrambled eggs for Cloud as they hadn't brought dog food for him. They had fed him their leftover picnic supplies the night before.

They dine in the lush Egyptian cotton terry robes provided. Sean goes as far as to pull out a chair for Cloud and seat him at the table.

"Oh my God, you are not doing that!" Laura protests. "No, he is not allowed at the table."

Cloud who has been reticent to take Sean up on his offer, remains on the ground where he sits and whines.

"They do it in France," Sean protests mildly.

Nice try guy, but I knew she wouldn't go for it. Cloud pushes against Sean to thank him, wagging his tail, and dutifully awaits being served his plate on the ground as usual.

"You are going to have that dog so spoiled he will become unbearable."

"But he's special, he can see ghosts."

"Yes, he's special, but that's not the point. He is one of the most well-behaved dogs I have ever seen, and I will not have you ruin him!"

Laura checks herself. *Why am I being so bitchy? Maybe because I'm terrified!*

She revises her sharp tone. "I'm sorry, we cannot spoil him that way."

Sean looks at her as if to say this is the first time, I've ever seen you raise your voice.

"Is the honeymoon over already?" he cracks.

"Oh gosh no. I am a bit edgy."

"I see that. Why don't you relax and drink your coffee?" He had ordered it just the way she likes it, a double shot with a splash of almond milk

"These blueberry muffins are to die for."

"Would you like to have a massage before we head back this morning?

"Uh, yes, that would be amazing."

Sean picks up his phone and orders a double massage for them in their quarters.

"It's done. They'll be here in about 30 minutes," he reports.

"I'd like them to set their tables up out here. It's private enough and the fountain is soothing."

"I don't see why not." Sean holds up both his arms as if he is surrendering to something horrific. "Let the princess have her way is my motto."

Something about his comment, his words reminding her of someone she couldn't remember, triggers something in her that wants to sabotage the moment, but she holds fast and keeps her mouth shut trying her best to soak it all in.

Boy, do I need to call Michelle. She will bring me back down to reality.

Time Will Tell

"Maybe we could catch a meeting before we get back to the Crescent. Do you mind looking one up while I drive?"

"You look pale." Sean looks at her. "I think a meetin' might be a good idea."

"Yea, I'm a little, uh, overwhelmed I guess." She studies the astonishing ring on her finger. It has been cleaned and polished. The blue diamond is clear while harboring a smoky shadow to the overall color giving the ring a sense of mystery. The canary marquise diamonds, nestled on either side, radiate with light as if sunlight has been captured within them.

"We've never been to a meeting together before."

"Well, it's probably not the best idea on a continuin' basis, but it won't hurt occasionally," he reassures her.

"I should be nervous too, but I'm not." He takes her hand and squeezes it. His hand is warm and the pressure of his touch reassuring. *A normal person would feel good about the devotion this man has for me, but if I learned anything, I'm not normal.*

They find a noon meeting in the town of Napa. They only have to wait about 20 minutes before it starts.

"Should we ask if Cloud can go in?" Sean asks her.

"Well, I don't like leaving him here in the car alone with the top down, but he needs to guard the car."

"Someone could steal him?"

Laura laughs, "I'd like to see them try."

That's right Laura Boo, I would eat the man alive who would try to steal me!

"Nevertheless, let's put the top up."

"Done."

The usual suspects start showing up. The whole world has given up smoking, but smokers are always prevalent outside the door of a meeting, despite the NO SMOK-ING sign posted on the door.

There are a dozen or more attendees seated in fold-ing chairs forming a circle. The leader starts the sharing going clockwise and when they get to Sean, he tells ev-eryone he has just proposed to the "hotttie sittin' next to him." The group responds with laughter.

Then it is Laura's turn, and she wants to pass, but Mi-chelle says now that she has almost 6 months sobriety, she should always try to share. "Because that's how you learn, listening to that ego of yours all by yourself ain't gonna' cut it." The words ring in her ears as if Michelle is present.

"Hi, I'm Laura, an alcoholic." *How many times have I said that and yet I've never said it here? I know these people aren't judging me, but still it is hard to let go of the shame.*

"As Sean just told you, we are making a commitment to each other. I might not ever be ready for the commit-ment, but I love him and since he asked, and went out of his way to make our time together special, I have said yes." She looks over at him to see how that lands on him. *He seems fine with the truth.* She continues. "I'm not at the point in my sobriety that I trust myself entirely to make sound decisions. I do trust Sean though and he travels a lot, so I said yes, because I don't know when I will see him next." Several people chuckle. "We have had an incredible couple of days together. That's all I've got. Just trying to stay in the now." She squeezes his hand while waves of heat wash over her. *Maybe I was too honest. Is he offended?*

Later back in the car. Sean asks her if he is being too pushy. They have left the top up and it is much easier to talk without the wind blowing the words out of their mouths.

"No, but we don't have to do this thing right away." Searching his expressions, she waits for him to reply.

"Of course not. I will let you determine the when and where, though I had my hopes up for Scotland in August."

"Oh Sean, this is all so new, let's not put a time into the equation just yet."

Distractions

Chad Owens has taken Sean's words to heart and has booked a room at the Crescent for the next couple of days.

"Maybe you could meet him for breakfast without me. I'm running late," Laura says, putting on her running shoes.

"Late for what?" Sean frowns and puts his hands on his hips like a football referee signaling encroachment.

"I've got to take Cloud out."

"I already took him."

"Oh," *Damn!*

"So, what is your problem all of a sudden with Chad?"

"Nothing, you're going to talk shop and I've got work to do. You look at me like I'm weaseling out."

"No, no I understand. You're right. I'll check with you later."

Laura grabs a muffin and some juice and sits down to write. She has recently started the second book of *The Two Moons of Merth* that tells the story of the descendants of Aadya and Poma.

With all the distractions Laura finds herself again getting further and further behind. Stuart has read most of what she has so far and thought there was a possibility for a movie option. "But you have to get your ass in gear," he had warned her. "I'm glad you're happy and busy having a life. But I swear to God if you don't wrap up this project soon…"

It happened on a night so still the smoke from the fires blew straight up. The flames had all been stoked with ash-

es for the long hours of peaceful rest. The anomaly began with the most wonderous display of cascading lights. There were brilliant blues, tangerine oranges, chartreuse, reds dark and moody, blinding whites. The colors coiled across the night sky were bright enough to awaken almost everyone except those exhausted by too much work or too much drink.

Cloud jumps up and rubs against Laura's leg, then begins to paw with his right front paw like he is identifying a ghost. He does this several times a day now while the crew is here. It's as if they stir up the ghosts more. So, Laura doesn't pay too much attention to him.

I like this. Another hundred pages and I will be finished.

But Cloud continues to create a disturbance circling in a manic display. She takes her phone and videos him and sends it to Sean.

...Take my laptop out and put the headset on Cloud. U know what to do...

I do? I guess I've watched him enough times. I can handle this. "Come here, Cloud let's put the ears on." Cloud lowers his head obligingly and she struggles to right the laptop screen in order to see what all the mysterious footwork is about. A chill spreads across the room like the patio door has blown open, but it latched. There is a dark-complected pregnant woman on the screen, and she seems distraught. Laura looks again toward the French doors to see if they have blown open, and there is, a reflection in the windowpanes of the door, the same woman she sees on the screen. *What am I seeing here?*

She looks again and the image flutters and waves, but it is still there. Then she sees a pair of pale hands encircle the woman's neck and choke her. She looks on the screen and the same thing is happening there. A pulse of electricity runs down her body like a thousand needlepoints, Laura falls to floor and drops the laptop.

Cloud leaps to her side and starts barking incessantly, but no one is coming. No one knows Laura is lying there on the floor. He goes over to the front door and pulls on the door handle. It opens a little, but then blows back shut. *What the hell is that?* He sees a menacing shadow trying to hold the door shut and when he looks around, he sees an apparition of a man wearing an old-fashioned hat. He tries again and this time before it shuts, he uses his nose and front left paw to push it open wider so he can escape.

The door slams shut behind him. Cloud immediately picks up Sean's scent and follows it to the elevator. He stops and whines. *I can't get on that freaking thing unless someone pushes the button. Wait a minute, I can push the button.* Cloud leaps up and punches the single button, the antiquated elevator bangs and bumps up its way to the shaft opening and slides open, but the collapsible scissor gate is too tricky. *I might get lucky and get it open, but I'll never get it shut. Pretty sure it won't run if the gate isn't latched. I'll take the stairs and try to pick up his scent again.*

At each floor Cloud goes over to the nearby elevator shaft and checks for Sean's smell. *Nothing. Maybe I'm overthinking this. I heard him say something about breakfast. Wish I had paid more attention.* The anxiety is flooding Cloud's normally rational mind. He tears down the rest of the stairwell and races into the dining room where he knows he's not supposed to go for some reason he has never understood. *My paws are cleaner than most people's shoes. I'm not sure why they don't want me in there. Maybe they think I'm going to make a big, gigantic, stinky poop or lift my leg or something. Ignorance, that's all it is.* Despite all the smells of omelets and bacon, maple syrup, butter and juice, Cloud picks up Sean's scent almost immediately. *He and some guy are over there in the corner near the window.* Cloud races across the expansive dining room filled with linen covered round tables while some of the breakfasters do a double take of the big white dog running past.

When Sean sees Cloud, he jumps up out of his seat. "Cloud, what are you doing here?" Cloud barks once loud enough to cause a break in the jumbled conversations of dozens of guests who stop talking long enough to stare. Sean throws his linen napkin on the table. "Cloud, what is it? What are you trying to tell me?"

Cloud pushes on his leg and heads toward the lobby and the elevator, pausing only once to make sure Sean follows. A dazed Chad traipses along too. *I better go to the elevator and wait. They'll never follow me up the stairs.*

"What in the world is going on chum?" Cloud barks sharply at the door of the elevator and Sean punches the button. The elevator arrives and the ride seems to drag on as Cloud anxiously whines nonstop until they finally arrive at the eighth floor.

Sean struggles to find his key. When they do get inside, Laura is sitting up on the couch looking a little stunned with Nanu's ghost next to her hugging her and patting her leg.

"Laura, are you, all right?" He sits down beside her right where Nanu was sitting.

"Uh yeah, I don't quite know what happened." I texted you and got out the headset as you suggested. Um, then I was looking at it onscreen, when I actually saw the image of the woman reflected in the glass of the veranda door. I saw a man reach in and try to strangle her. It's all so crazy."

Sean picks the laptop up from off the floor. "It should be recorded. Let's take a look." The three of them look at the video repeatedly. They all see the pregnant woman in her modest tiny floral print dress and her open three quarter-sleeved sweater, as a man wearing a gray pin-stripe suit and wingtip shoes approaches her from behind. There are some muffled noises of Laura falling on the floor.

"I hate to be an alarmist," Chad clears his throat, "but we may have an Etheric Revenant here." He looks at Sean. "I know you like to stick to science, but, and this is mostly legend, although I've witnessed it. There are those that believe people who are murdered, or die of tragic circumstances, will try to make contact." Sean nods subtly.

"Let's not go there just yet."

"I actually saw her reflection in the French door!"

Cloud goes to his head set and paws at it.

"Right, boy. We should take a look." As soon as they are up and running, they see Nanu in the room. She has a worried look on her face.

"Why can't ghosts just use sign language to communicate?" Laura asks.

"That's an extremely good question," Sean tells her looking up from the computer. "I've seen thousands of ghosts and not one of them has ever tried that. Actually, for the most part they seem unaware of us. It's only when there is a close connection to relatives that we see anything close to interaction, but then they limit their time with relatives as if they are protecting them from something we can't see. Like radiation or something even though we don't see measurable amounts." Sean's voice trails off as he sinks into his thoughts.

"It's hot in here," Laura goes over to the French doors and opens them. The fog still hangs low over the bay.

"Why would I have fainted?" The two men look at each other and shrug.

"Low blood sugar?" Chad teases her.

"Well, I don't want my home to become a magnet for wayward evil spirits," she complains.

Sean looks at the floor for a minute and then at Laura. His smile disarms her. "Well, give that up sweetheart, this place is loaded with paranormal activity."

Sean looks at his phone for the time. "Chad and I need to get with the crew. If you don't want to come join us, you ought to at least get out of here for a little while."

Laura lets out a short gust of breath. "I'm fine, you guys get out of here. I'm going to write for a while and then I'll take Cloud out for a break." She waves them on.

Evil Spirits Explained

It takes the crew nearly a day to get everyone loaded and into the bus.

"I would like to see you sooner than later," Sean tells Laura as they say their goodbyes on the veranda watching as the bus below gets loaded with people and equipment. He tangles his fingers in hers asking a question of her with his disarming green eyes and she struggles as if there might be an answer. "I'm going to have Melissa set up my calendar to share it with you. I know we're stateside for the next two months then we head to Europe. Scotland is scheduled for early August." Her emotions flood her brain and pool in places not built to absorb them. *Dammit, I'm not going to cry!*

"How the heck do you get all this gear to Europe?" She blurts out deflecting her anxiety, with what she hopes sounds like naïve impunity.

Recognizing her fear, Sean jumps topic with her.

"We usually scale down to only one bus. Everyone carries their own gear and if we need to rent stuff we do. It's not such a big deal."

"I didn't want to tell you this, but I'm going to anyway."

"What? You're not going to break my heart, are you? After I paid for that expensive ring?" They both laugh.

"Yeah right." She gives him an annoyed look.

"What then?"

"I don't want you to judge me, but ever since I had that incident with that evil spirit in my suite. I've been sort of creeped out."

"I understand completely. I've been there myself. I've often wondered how these ghosts, especially now that we can see them, affect us if they are all around us. And you, my dear, live in a place where there are many."

"I know. With you here it's one thing, but alone, I'm not sure I will be as brave. I get these creepy feelings now that are unexplainable." Sean gives her words credence with his full focus.

"You probably are developing more sensitivity to the apparitions. Our friend Chad could probably be of some assistance. Would you mind if I asked him to stick around for a few more days?"

"You think he would be interested in that?"

"Are you kiddin'? This place is full of ghosts, that's like crack to him. I tell you what. I will leave my laptop and Cloud's headset here so you two will have some tools to work with."

"But isn't that equipment expensive?

"Nah, it was the development of the software that was expensive, more like $300,000. That's just a fancy Apple laptop and, well, I guess the headset is valuable. Anyway," he shrugs. "I can either go without, or they can expense another set for me."

"You sure? I'll only keep it if Owens agrees to stay, and I can always send it to you."

"Sure. Let me try to reach him before he takes off." Owens agrees to meet Laura at her suite in half an hour.

"Good-bye my sweetheart. I will call you tonight." Laura grabs another hug and holds tight.

"It's a good thing we're doing this," she tells him. "I'll see you soon."

"So, thanks for staying on a couple of days." Laura tells Chad as she invites him in. "Can I get you something?"

"Probably not. It's a little early to hit the sauce."

Mmm...that's an invitation to cave if I've ever heard one.

He waves his hand as if he is joking. "I've done some more thinking and it may be possible what we are dealing with here is what we call a 'sensed presence' in the trade. You spend a lot of time alone in your suite, don't you?

"Sure."

"And are you under any kind of stress?"

"Well, the fact that Sean and I just got engaged...I would call that stressful. And he just left me again."

Chad gives Laura an understanding look. "There is an environmental psychologist, Peter Suedfeld who has studied and written a lot about this topic. His theory is that we spend most of our time processing external stimuli from the world around us. Persistent exposure to stimuli we are evolutionarily unprepared to process, may manifest by us focusing more within ourselves. That's a fancy way of saying our subconscious self is mysteriously amazing."

"But the woman was recorded exactly as I saw her."

"Yes, of course." He mulled this over for a minute. "I've got to admit I am still trying to wrap my mind around this new technology. What I am proposing here, is that your state of mind might have been the magnet for the 'sensed presence.' History is full of such sightings.

"Joshua Slocum, the first person to circumnavigate the earth single-handedly, swore he had a conversation with the pilot of Columbus's ship the Pinta when he was ill with food poisoning and riding out a terrible storm. It's also well documented that grieving individuals who have lost a spouse often experience a visit from their deceased partner.

"Since we have this sighting recorded, we can't rule this theory out. Am I to understand there was never a murder committed here in the hotel?"

"Not to my knowledge."

"Then I propose the apparition was attracted to your isolation and fear."

"Hhmm…sounds plausible."

Owens shrugs, "perhaps this phenomenon even explains God as experienced in the Old Testament. I don't know."

"What do you mean? There's plenty of evidence to suggest there is a God."

"How so?"

"Just look around. People didn't create this earth and all the life on it. We know how to destroy it, but we can't create it."

"You could be right, my dear, I didn't mean to get into an existential argument about God."

"I guess the best analogy I've ever heard was in one of Mary Karr's memoirs when her friend, author Tobias Wolff, tells her not believing in God is like not believing in Bob Dylan because you've only heard his CD's and haven't seen him live in concert."

Owens chuckles and looks a little bit puzzled by her advocacy. "I didn't mean to offend."

"No, that's okay a lot of alcoholics don't believe in God. I just happen to be one that does." *Oops, didn't mean to go there.*

Owens tilts his head and studies her as if he was finally connecting the dots. "Ooh, that's why Wilson wasn't drinking the other day at the vineyard. You got him to quit."

"Well, actually it's more the other way around. I didn't mean to break his anonymity."

"Well shit, I should probably quit myself, but I don't want to."

Laura laughs, "No one does, that's not how it works." She touches him gently on the shoulder. "The joke is we're saving a chair for you down at AA. Whenever you're ready we'll be there."

"Seriously you just quit?"

"Not without a whole lot of resistance and more help. I'd be glad to take you to a meeting."

"Mmm, no, I'll be having a beer with one of those incredible Reubens your restaurant serves here in a short while." He looks to see what time it is. It's just 10:45.

"Well, keep on drinking and when it gets to be too much you won't know it, but the people around you will."

"Then I'm in big trouble as I don't have many people around anymore. My wife left me years ago and my daughter barely speaks to me."

"See there, it may be time for you."

"Hmm, I doubt it, I'm nearly 70 years old."

"Never too late," her voice trails off. *How solid is my resolve? Do I have it in me to stay sober?*

191

A Chilling Encounter

"So, why don't you pull that laptop out and let's look at that sighting again." Chad tells Laura, "And while we're at it we could go ahead and hook your dog, ah, Cloud is it? up to the headset."

Laura picks up Sean's knapsack which so recently had been in his hands. She can still smell him on the drab green canvas. Rubbing her hand across the worn leather clasp, where his hand had flipped it open many times, sends her deeper into her sensory recall.

Cloud's ears perk up when he sees her open the backpack. He has been pouting for most of the morning since Sean left. She flips open the silver Mac and searches for the most recent file. *That's not it.*

It takes a little more searching but then she finds the file of the woman being choked. The shadowy figure is lurking in the drapes, a detail she had not noticed before. She glances over at the now billowing sheers mounted on the French doors and considers getting rid of them. *It's not like anyone can see in here anyway through those doors. Maybe I should consider redecorating a bit.*

"Here let's sit down," she says to Chad pointing to the barstools at the granite counter. She clears some space by sliding aside a couple of books and a notebook, one that Sean had, just this morning, been taking notes on. His handwriting is bold and almost illegible.

They play the short video several times. "This is definitely ominous," Chad admits.

"So, what you were saying before is that this could actually be a manifestation of my stress about my commitment to Sean?"

"No, not exactly. I don't mean to say it is your hallucination. I'm saying it may be your anxiety is what is attracting this apparition. We don't know who she was or why she was here, but it is your state of mind that might have played a hand in this. She's being strangled and you are metaphorically being choked by your apprehensions. There's no doubt in my mind this woman was strangled to death, but we don't know if she lived here or even visited this hotel while she was alive."

Chad looks at Laura as if to apologize for something. "Maybe we can actually see them now with Wilson's wild ass invention, but we are on the cusp, and don't really have an understanding of what's going on.

"I'm extremely interested in what your dead Grandmother may have to tell us though. If she can." He reaches toward her. "Laura, hand me that thing. I want a go at this."

Laura fits the wireless headset on Cloud and hands Owens the laptop. It doesn't take long before they have a sighting of Nanu.

"What if I could train Cloud to give me a signal when he sees Nanu?"

Owens turns toward her and grins, "I think that would be a marvelous idea,"

"It needs to be a signal that is easily distinguishable. He already knows a few tricks Daisy's trainer taught him. "Cloud, when you see this woman," she points to the screen where Nanu is visible. "I want you to ...bark twice. Can you do that for me?"

Well sure Toots. I'm amazing, I can do that. Woof, woof! *Now let's have some of those treats I like.* Cloud breaks rank and heads for the drawer in the kitchen where the treats are stored.

"Of course," Laura reassures him and follows him into the kitchen.

When she gets back to Chad, he is glued to the computer screen. "I want you to do something silly."

"What's that?'

"I want you to look directly at your grandmother and ask her help us solve the mystery of the pregnant woman being strangled. Let's see what her response is."

"But Sean said we cannot expect interaction, especially if it's someone she never knew."

"I know, I know. Let's just pretend we don't know any better. Let's be flexible."

There was that window shade that rolled up suddenly in the attic that time, and we've seen her point and gesture.

"Okay." Looking at the image on the screen Laura turns toward where her grandmother's image should be located in relation to Cloud's vision. "Nanu, we want this bad ghost to go away. Who is she? I don't want her here in the hotel. Can you help me get rid of her?"

Nanu, who at this moment is appearing in what looks like a vintage '50s dress and gloves, does not respond at first. In fact, she appears to be staring out into space.

"Nothing."

"Wait a minute," Chad tells her as he fans his hand at her. They stand motionless and watch for some time, but nothing happens. It's as if Nanu is in a trance.

"Nanu, can you give us a sign you can hear me?

With that the patio door creaks open as if someone has unlatched it. A flutter then a dark shadow falls across the floor so insipidly Laura is uncertain if she saw it or imagined it. Every pore in her body opens and a consolidated chill rips across her bare skin. Cloud growls softly and bares his teeth.

"Shh." Chad takes his finger to his lips and turns to caution Laura, but she hears nothing. Then suddenly there is a crash out on the veranda. Cloud leaps up and rushes out to see what it is. Laura and Chad are right behind him, Chad still has the laptop in his hands, and they can see a blinding light on the screen. Other than that they can see nothing on the veranda itself. Cloud growls menacingly and his hackles go up. Then nothing. "Whatever that was," says Chad, "it's gone now."

Setting a Date

It takes Laura another six weeks to finally finish her manuscript. Stuart is satisfied and off her back.

"I don't know what to do with myself," she admits to Michelle one day when they are having coffee. They both have begun to regularly attend the meeting in the basement of St. Bartholomew's on Saturdays and often go for coffee afterward. "Now the book is done, I want to take a break," Laura says as they sit down in the courtyard of the coffee shop.

"Seems to me you oughta' start planning a trip to Scotland and a little shindig to tie the knot."

"I know… I know. I just can't bring myself to make those phone calls."

"What phone calls?"

"For starters to my parents and friends. First though, we have to set a date. Sean has been bugging me to do that so he can make a reservation. He wants to rent a castle for God's sakes!"

"Hmm, I need to be coming to that celebration."

"Would you?"

"You bet your sweet ass."

"Okay, then help me figure this out."

"Pull out your phone and let's look at your calendar."

"Oh, right now?"

Michelle gives her a bored contemptuous look. "Yes, right now girl. You gonna' put this off and lose your man if you don't get with it."

"Oh, Sean would wait for me forever."

"You shor' about that?"

He would! I know he would.

"Let's look at his calendar first, with the book finished, I'm completely free."

Michelle studies Laura who is fumbling with her phone as if there is a road map in there she can follow.

"Look, the last two weeks of the shooting schedule are open. He's already set that time aside."

"Imagine that," Michelle says. "That makes it easy. Now call him."

"I'll do that later."

"No ma'am, I've got to get my plane ticket."

"So, you're really coming?"

"Hell yes."

"I'll call him later. He likes me to Facetime."

"You can do that here. It's time I got to meet the man if I'm coming to his castle wedding."

With the stealth of an odorless gas, joy seeps into Laura's veins, then gurgles up flooding her whole body. *I am actually planning a wedding. There is a man in my life I love.*

"You are something else," she tells Michelle while secretly pleased by her helpful insistence.

"Well, yes I am, but let's not get distracted from our mission."

Laura leans into the phone in the bright sunlight. "We're going to have to move into the shade to see."

"That's fine," Michelle pops up to assess the situation, but most of the shady spots have been taken. She points, "Over there by the wall, that'll work."

Laura's limbs grow heavy as she scoots away from the table. Her heart pounds and her mind glazes with doubt.

The new chairs are cold to the touch, but she sits down anyway.

"You okay?" Michelle asks her.

Laura slips her a weak smile. "Of course, I am," She says and punches the #1 favorite on her phone.

But Sean doesn't answer. Instead a young woman's face appears on the screen. "Sean's phone this is Marcia." Her accent is British and matter of fact.

What the f***?

"Oh, hi Laura, Sean asked me to carry his phone for him, he's been climbing all over some scaffolding and he was afraid it would fall out of his pocket. We haven't met yet. Would you like to talk with him?"

Yeees, that's why I called, bitch! She wants to shout, but instead Laura sucks it up and says, "Yes," cheerfully. Happily, like the bride she is going to be.

Laura looks at Michelle who is reading her emotions like a graphic novel and is softly smiling to nurture levity. "Don't make shit up," Michelle warns in soft deep tones.

After a few minutes Sean is procured. Laura is still stuffing her feelings like a suicidal parachutist down the hole of her self-proclaimed emergency.

"Hey babe, what's up?" Just hearing his voice sets her at ease.

"Oh, sorry, I should have texted but I'm here with Michelle and we were looking at your August schedule. What do you think about August 26th for a wedding?"

There. The words slip out like anxious water. Michelle is grinning at her like they are two teens calling a boy, encouraging her with animated expressions.

"Oh wow, that would be wonderful!"

"We can talk about it tonight or when you are not busy."

"I'm clowning around helping the guys here set up. It's no big deal. So, what's next?"

"We need to pick out the location and invite people."

"I'll have Melissa check out some ideal locations and narrow it down a bit."

"That's fine, I'll start looking too, but Sean…"

"Yes, Laura."

"I don't want this getting too big. I'm thinking close family and friends and your crew alone must be 30 people."

"The crew is currently at 28, and Wilson Enterprises is now close to 50. They will <u>all</u> want to come."

Fifty employees! The man chasing ghosts is in way over his head.

"Of course. Send me your list when you get a chance to have Melissa pull it together."

"Wow, I'm pumped. Talk to you later, I've got to go."

The last thing Laura sees is the side of Sean's head as he has already engaged in another conversation." *He is like a distracted boy with too many toys to play with.*

"Bye," her word lingers in the air as she joins the Michelle back in the world of real.

"Good job! That wasn't difficult now was it?"

"No, I should have texted him first. He was busy. I didn't get to introduce you."

"Aww, don't make too much of that," Michelle flaps her hand nonchalantly at Laura.

"So which castle would you choose?" Laura asks Cloud as she peruses Scottish Castles available for weddings on her laptop. Cloud is curled next to her on the couch with his buttery fur tickling her bare legs. He does not engage with the computer screen ever, even when they are using it to see Nanu, or any of the other apparitions in the hotel.

Of all the places to get married nothing could be more romantic than a Scottish castle. And this lands in my lap. Well, Laura pretty much everything about your life has been this way. How did I get to be so privileged when others struggle just for food and shelter?

Cloud barks twice as he has been trained to do when he sees Nanu, who has curled up on the opposite side of Laura. She squeezes her granddaughter affectionately. And Laura, unknowingly, scrolls back to Achnagairn Castle near Inverness. *Can't pronounce it but has enough rooms for all the guests on the property and a magnificent ballroom for the wedding itself.*

Cloud's Perspective

"Stuart, I'm giving you advance notice as you start putting a book tour into motion. Cloud laying in the sun, curls his right front paw into his reach and licks it several times. *The phone is always a little baffling. I can't smell the other person and where they've been.*

"We hope you can be there, of course. You started this whole thing.

"Yes, I prefer not to get on the road before late September.

"I guess I could do one book signing before I leap over to Scotland.

"That would be cool to have the two of us on a talk show right after the wedding. We need to allow at least two weeks for us to get away. You know, have a honeymoon.

"I don't know, probably somewhere in Europe. We'll be there anyway.

"I'll send you Melissa's contact info and your scheduler can talk to her.

"I'll have Cloud with me, so please tell her to make arrangements for assisting me with his care. *What was that?* Cloud's ears stand at attention. *Laura tells me I'm going to Scotland, too, and this time I will have to travel on the plane.*

"I suppose he could be in the interview. I think that's a great idea."

"You want to do what? That's not necessary I don't need a stylist. I have tons of clothes."

Cloud watches Laura talking on the phone as she paces erratically around the suite and when she pauses, she tugs at her pants.

Nanu comes into the kitchen and sits down on one of the counter stools. "Woof, woof!" *There, I barked twice to let her know Nanu is here and she doesn't notice. She does not get me a treat! What's up with her anyway?*

"Not now, Cloud. Let me think." Laura hangs up and tosses her phone on the counter. Then goes into the bedroom where her closet, a room almost as large as the kitchen, houses Laura's pants and a million other things. Cloud follows. *I like it in here. It's cozy and the smells from the street linger on the clothing.* Laura pulls off the pants she wore this morning when they went running. She stares into the mirror wall. Then frowns.

Don't really know what's going on with Laura but I love the mirror. I can see how pretty I am. Fine looking fellow.

"I have to get my act together and figure out what to take," she tells me. *As if I care.*

She takes clothing down she never wears and holds garments by the hanger up to her shoulders pressing her forearm across the middle of the garment onto her body. Frowning, she strips down to her underwear and occasionally tries something on, deepening her frown if it is too tight or ill-fitting. If that happens, she tosses it into a pile in the corner of the closet. *Thanks Laura, I like snuggling in your clothes.*

This goes on for a while then she goes back to the kitchen to get her phone. I follow her though I have created a comfy little nest of clothes in the corner.

"Just don't drink today Laura," *I am surprised to hear her say this. I did not know this is still an issue. Maybe I should be more concerned.*

"Hey Tessa"

"I know I don't blame you. I've been crazy busy finishing the book. And there's a lot going on here at the hotel."

"Has it been that long?

"I did return your calls.

"I guess I was scared to tell you I quit drinking.

"At least I've told you about Sean. Right?

"Well, shit, we do have a lot to catch up on.

"Okay, I can do lunch. Tomorrow? Where?"

Hanging up Laura dials Stuart back. "I don't know what I was thinking. I can use all the help I can get. Go ahead and have a stylist contact me."

Just Don't Drink Today

"Hey girl, you look great," Tessa gets up from her chair and hugs Laura.

"You do, too. Sorry I've been such a negligent friend," She says as she pulls out her chair and sits at the glass table.

"Well, it's not okay, but I heard through the grapevine you had sobered up." Tessa takes a sip of the dark red wine in her long-stemmed glass, not grasping the irony of her actions. "I mean it's not okay that I haven't heard from you in so long. The other thing, you sobered up. Good for you," she says, thinking that another drinking buddy bites the dust.

Just don't drink today, Laura. This is exactly why I've been avoiding her. Laura takes a big gulp of the water from the sweating glass at her place setting. Her mouth is especially dry and the wine...*I can smell it on her breath from here.*

"So, you got your invitation?"

"Yes, but I don't think I'll be able to get time off."

"Oh, that's too bad. It will be quite a party."

"How do you even have a wedding without champagne?" Tessa asks.

"What?"

"You know the bubbly stuff? Have you already forgotten?"

"No, of course not. There will be champagne for our guests. Sean and I don't drink alcohol. That doesn't mean we won't serve it."

"Just sayin'" Tessa glances at her nails. Laura is trying to remember why they had been friends for so long.

"The castle is gorgeous. You ought to reconsider. It will be Scotland in August for God's sake."

"You know I'd love to, but I don't have that much vacation time right now."

Well that was stressful. I guess I need to follow my instincts more often. There is a reason I haven't hung out with Tessa since I got sober. Maybe I am changing for the better. Laura jumps into her silver and black Mini Cooper and tries to phone Michelle, but she's not answering.

Off to the Races

"Why don't you meet me in New York, and you can help me pick out my wedding gown before we head for Scotland," Laura tells her mother. She has finally gotten her trained to Facetime call her. "I've had them book the Ritz Carlton for me because they have butlers for your room, and I'll have Cloud with me, so I'll need that personal service. And it's right across the street from Central Park."

"You're taking Cloud?"

"Yes, he's a big part of this deal you know. He's famous. My God, now that the FilmFlix pilot aired, people are coming to the hotel just to see him. I have to schedule our appearances like he was some damn duck in Memphis."

"What are you talking about?"

"The Peabody ducks. Surely, you've heard of them.

"No, I guess not."

"You'll have to Google it then."

"Anyway, I'm doing interviews before and after the wedding, and Cloud will be part of them. And of course, he'll be in our ceremony."

"Laura, I'm enormously excited about this. I'd love to help you shop for the dress, but isn't that something you should do before then?"

"Well, maybe, but I can't resist the thought of getting it in New York."

"What about alterations?"

"I don't think that will be a big problem. Out of all the bridal stores in Manhattan, surely I should be able to find one dress that fits perfectly."

"You have become such a free spirit since you moved out West."

"Not really."

Pressing forth with her cheerfulness Emily tells her daughter, "I'm all in...can't wait. We love Sean. He's perfect for you."

That's scary. She's gushing. "So, I'll see you guys in a few weeks then."

"Yes, looking forward to it Laura. The whole thing will be such an adventure. Text me your travel dates for everything so I can coordinate. We'll try to book a room near yours. Your father will be glad to babysit Cloud while we shop." Emily is smiling in a way she hasn't done in years. "See you in New York."

This is becoming a family affair. I can actually stand my parents now that I am sober. Those 'oldtimers' in AA told me I would change.

Traveling with Cloud has turned into a big damn deal. Little children want to pet him, and everybody wants to stop and talk. *I've gotten more notoriety from Cloud than I ever dreamed of as an author. It's amazing how many people have already seen the FilmFlix episode.*

Wading through LaGuardia is treacherous enough without trying to get Cloud to a place he can pee after the long flight. *It's like all the huddled masses are conjoining in one enormous whirl of humanity.* Oddly, it was Liam who suggested Laura not book a direct flight allowing for Cloud to have a break in Dallas. Despite this it was still stressful. *Luckily, I figured out to 'go' on the plane before deboarding. I don't know what I would have done if I hadn't. I couldn't possibly leave him alone at the bathroom door. Though he would fiercely resist, someone might be tempted to snatch him. Well, I guess I could have taken him into the stall with me. That would be a sight! I wish I had gotten someone to travel with me. Just who would that have been? The wedding is still 10 days off. 10 Days! Holy SHIT!* Laura finally sees signage for the pet relief station and veers off from the stream of human traffic.

The stench from the pet station hits them full in the face as Laura pulls open the door.

Cloud balks. *Another plastic grass pee spot. Nasty! Just get me to a real tree please.*

"I know you don't like it Cloud, but tonight I'll take you walking in Central Park. You will love that. And tomorrow the parents come."

He doesn't even lift a leg, just squats like a puppy. Laura rinses down the pee mat with the hose provided and they edge out into the flowing crowd. *Thank God Stuart is sending a car, all I have to do now is follow the throng to baggage claim and look for a sign with my name on it.*

"Hello, Ms. Haskell" a young man with slicked back red hair and freckles wearing a chauffer's uniform walks up to her at baggage claim. He is wielding a superfluous sign with her name on it.

"Oh, hello. How did you know it was me?"

"Because that's Cloud with you." The kid shifts his eyes downward. "I'd recognize him anywhere."

"Oh right."

"I've got three bags."

"Just let me know when they come around, and I'll pull them out."

"Sure, there's one now. That royal blue one." *I've had that suitcase for decades. It's taken me lots of places. And now this. On to Scotland we shall go.*

911

The elevator ride up 70 flights is much different than at home in the Crescent. *Nothing like being vaulted like a bone toward the sky! I don't know how to protect Laura in this strange place.*

"I'm exhausted Cloud. I'll order us something in and we'll get to Central Park after dinner. I've brought your special food. I don't want you overindulging while we travel."

CRAP! I bet I can still get some morsels out of her.

The phone rings and it is Stuart checking on Laura's safe arrival. "This trip is a little different than the last time I came here. Thank you for being part of my recovery team."

"Now Laura, I merely saw the storm that was brewing."

"Maybe so, but you started putting the squeeze on me, and you were extremely patient while I took months off from my work to get sober."

"You would have done the same for me."

"Well, let's hope I never have to. Getting sober is no picnic."

"Anyway, moving on," Laura can almost hear him fidget over the phone. "Your interview is day after tomorrow."

"Yes, I've got it in my calendar. Tomorrow mother and I are going to go shopping for a wedding dress, and Friday we head for Scotland."

"Don't forget I was the one who introduced you two. Who knew, right?"

"Yes, who knew. I thought I was done with love."

"Laura, no one is ever done with love, my dear."

Wonder if that's true?

"A car will pick you up at 10 sharp. Be ready."

"You're going to think you died and went to heaven, Cloud. Central Park is a special place." Cloud lifts his snout and let thousands of diverse scents fill his nostrils. Some are pungent decaying garbage smells, toxic fumes from the cacophony of speeding cars, the next second an overdose of perfume from a buxom woman walking past, booze breathe from another pedestrian, stinky, moldy, rat infested drains. The combined effect is like a ripe, pungent crust on a St. Andres cheese. Then a blast of drenched infused cuisine comes billowing out the door like sticky fog attached to two satisfied diners. *People with full stomachs smell distinctly different than hungry ones. Aah, is that hot dogs I smell? They sell them on the street here? How weird, yet delightful.*

As they cross through the frenetic traffic to get to the tree lined sidewalk, Cloud is surprised to see horses harnessed to open carriages. *I've seen those fellows before. They were always free in the fields. All distractions aside, I'm so glad to see trees and bushes and a little grass.* He tugs at his leash hoping Laura will get the memo and let him run a little. *Damn, it's been a long day.*

"No, Cloud you must heel. Even though it is a great forest here, you must stay on the leash until 9 p.m. That's what the doorman said. And there are places you are not allowed. I'm not sure where they are exactly. We'll probably be able to tell." Laura looks at her iWatch. Sean sent it to her just before she left, and she isn't used to it yet. Still, it was easier than pulling out her phone to tell the time. "Fifteen more minutes. Just hang on kiddo."

Cloud stops and does a double take as three illustrious cinnamon-colored Great Danes walk in unison down the sidewalk. *Wow look at those three! Those are the prissiest pack. I've never quite seen anything like it.* Laura takes the pause to stretch, the precursor to her running. *Yeah, let's get those kinks out and get a move on.* Cloud prances in place waiting for her to get mobile again. *This is sheer bliss after that crazy airplane trip.*

Soon, the two of them break into a run. They run and run and run. Laura is beginning to breathe hard when they reach the edge of a small lake. The sun has set, and path lights have tripped on. They both notice loose dogs, so Laura pulls out the ball toss.

Yippee!! Here I go!

After almost an hour of playing toss it is clear Laura has had enough. Cloud begs for just one more. She tosses it, and it flips over toward the edge of the lake and rolls into it before Cloud can snatch it up into his saliva-soaked jaws. Laura calls to him to come. *Damn, I can see it in the shadow of the water. I can almost reach it without jumping in.*

"Cloud, come!" Cloud breaks his focus on the brightly colored ball now muted by about nine inches of brown water. He looks up to see a group of thuggish youth approaching Laura.

"Hey lady you want some of this?" A tall scroungy teen wearing baggy pants, high top tennis shoes, and a skull cap is sidling up to Laura. He is grabbing his crotch and taunting her.

"Cloud, come!"

Adrenaline pumps, zinging every reflexive nerve through his body and Cloud leaps into action racing toward the offending marauder. He bares his teeth and growls aggressively. His body twitches with venomous hatred causing him to lose connection of all fours with the ground at times. One of the other teens tugs the ragged sleeve of the aggressor.

"C'mon don't be an asshole, Jax we've already been warned once tonight."

Jax clearly doesn't care what his friend is talking about and he takes another swig of whiskey from a greasy paper bag.

Laura wants to warn them that Cloud will attack if provoked, but his raucous snarling is too loud to shout over and, clearly, they are getting the message anyway. As a precaution she punches the 911 button on her new watch, barely confident that she knows what she is doing. She remembers going over that feature while setting it up. Then panic slaps her like a stinging blow across the face. *What if they pull a gun and shoot him?*

She decides interfering might confuse Cloud so she lets him do his thing, knowing that if he leaps at the kid, one of them will likely end up dead. The reasonable kid tugs a little harder. "Jax, you're drunk. Don't be a dick!"

"Yeah bro," one of the other three shadowy figures joins in. The two stragglers start backing away not sure who is more of a threat, the bully they shadow who they would have to answer to later, or the snarling animal.

Jax spins around despite Cloud's tectonic display and waves his arm randomly at them. "Get the fuck out of here you pussies, can't you see I'm busy here."

Seeing his opening Cloud leaps and attacks the offender from the back knocking him to the ground with such force he is temporarily dazed. All of the boys run in different directions like a burst of fireworks thwarted by a faulty fuse.

Oh shit! "Cloud stand down!" she shouts hoping he will obey. The lanky teen doesn't get up. Instead he lays there as if playing dead is the best option he has at the moment.

"Cloud! Come!" She walks at a safe distance past the mangy punk, but close enough to get a whiff of his boozy street stench.

"Now Cloud!" Seeing that is over for now. Cloud trots over to Laura's side looking back occasionally to make sure the offender doesn't follow them. Once they hit the next light pole Laura turns to make sure the asshole gets up. She sees him on all fours then she turns and marches toward the street where her panic melts into the noise of street sounds.

She stops to tell the doorman about the incident as a courtesy to the hotel more than anything, but it does give her a sense of relief to let someone know about her recent peril. The doorman is someone that can answer questions should the 911 alert harvest any takers.

"I'm sorry that happened to you ma'am, I will let the authorities know." She turns as she walks off. "Well, I wouldn't have been out there after dark, but it was the only way to get my dog a good run."

"He's a beautiful animal, looks like that dog on the *Ghosts Are Real* show."

She turns around and puts her index finger to her lips. "Shh." The doorman, accustomed to greeting celebrities, understands the code and winks at her surreptitiously.

"C'mon Cloud, time to get back and try out that fancy bed and see if it as good as they claim," she says casually reaching to graze the top of his head. She looks at her watch. It would be 3 a.m. in Scotland. She'd have to call Sean early in the morning.

Corned Beef and Baggage

Waking up, Laura peers down at the hallowed view of Central Park. The street is bustling with traffic, and the treetops, like large florets of broccoli, obscure where she and Cloud had their harrowing encounter the night before. Her parents plan to arrive by 9 a.m., in time for a full day of shopping. Room service is already knocking. Laura pulls on her new silk ivory robe, which matches the luxurious pajama set she is wearing. The ensemble, which feels like liquid against her skin, was recently purchased for this wedding trip.

She answers the door and takes the tray without letting the young man in, still feeling a little vulnerable from the night before. Cloud stands behind her with his ever-alert ears pointing forward.

"Hi, I also requested my dog be walked this morning."

"Yes, ma'am, do you have his leash?"

"Oh, you bring the food, and walk him?"

"Yes, ma'am. My name is Carlos, and I am your butler today."

"Well, this is Cloud and he's ready to go...literally," she says as she lets him in.

Carlos smiles and puts the back of his hand out for Cloud to sniff.

"Uh, we had an incident last night in the park. I wanted to let you know. He's normally quite even-tempered but he had to defend me last night, so he might be a little wary. Here take some of his puppy crack to give him, some now, and once you reach the park. He'll be ever devoted to you." Laura goes to the bedroom and reaches into her suitcase pocket for the baggie of treats and hands them to Carlos.

"Yes, ma'am, I'm sure we'll get along just fine."

"And Carlos, he's becoming recognized. So, please be careful and don't let people harass him, okay?

"Sure, I hear he is the dog from the *Ghosts are Real* show. I haven't seen it yet; I will have to watch it on You-Tube. My roommates and I don't have a TV."

"That's the one, he's gotten more famous than I am." *Eew, that sounded affected. I'm not famous except with book nerds.*

Laura opens the door and there stand her parents, baggage in hand, looking a little road weary after getting up at 5 a.m. to drive up from Falls Church. "Hi you guys!" She hugs her mother and then turns to her father. "Dad, it's been too long since I've seen you," she says giving him a tight hug. There is still a faint hint of his aftershave slapped on in the wee hours of the morning.

"We were talking about that in the car. The last time you visited was Thanksgiving two years ago."

"Oh my, and I was probably half toasted the whole time."

"Yes, you were. I am delighted you have finally figured things out," he says pulling at his ear. "You probably inherited the gene from my side of the family. Uncle Arthur went to an early grave because of his drinking."

"Oh, for heaven's sake, Vincent it's no one's fault," Emily sets down her over-sized handbag and turns to make her point.

"I'm just saying, there is a proven connection of hereditary predisposition."

"Guys there's lots to do. Our first appointment is in 20 minutes. It's down the street about a block we'll just walk, Mom."

"Yes, honey of course."

"What about the dog?" Vincent asks as Cloud, who has returned from his early morning walk, is now busy nosing him.

"Oh, we had an incident last night, I'll tell you about it later. I'm just going to have the hotel butler take care of him for the day. He's already been out this morning. Why don't you meet us for lunch somewhere, Dad?"

"Great, I'm going back to the room and take a nap. You guys phone me when you have a plan." He pecks Emily on the forehead and gives Laura a smile that says volumes. *He hasn't been around me sober since I was a little girl. He still doesn't trust me.*

"Great, we'll meet up for lunch somewhere. Get some rest."

As they march down the street New York style, Emily tells her mother, "They had a stylist help me prepare my wardrobe before I left, but I thought since you've been waiting forever for this day to come, you deserve to help me pick out the wedding dress."

"A stylist?" Emily gives her daughter a chagrined look. "My, you are privileged."

"I know it's totally annoying, but this is a big PR opportunity for the series and for me as a writer. Mostly it's because of who I am marrying and my dog, to tell you the truth."

"Well, it's sweet of you to share this moment with me. How much further?"

"Just another block, I think. I've got a list of our appointments on my phone, let me check the address."

Laura nods discreetly not wanting to point and look like a tourist. "Yes, it's up ahead."

The metallic clamor of the city streets is silenced as soon as the oversized glass door of the salon closes behind them. They are greeted by a young woman wearing black and white polka dot glasses with her long straight red hair pulled back tightly at the nape of her neck. Her slim body, black flats and painted on chemise feels very New York.

"You must be Laura and Emily. I'm Helen," she extends her hand with the affectation and rigidity of a drawbridge being lowered. "Your stylist sent us your measurements and explained your tight schedule, we have pulled some dresses and will have them modeled for you to better economize your time."

"Oh, that sounds terrific." They follow Helen who motions them into a private salon. And as if they are in a '50s sitcom, Helen snaps her fingers while another young woman comes out to confer with her in hushed tones.

"Please sit over here," Helen guides them to the white brocade love seat oozing with pillows. Though there are several other overstuffed choices to sit in, they squeeze in somewhat awkwardly together.

"We've prepared mimosas for you."

Laura laughs, "Well, give me the orange juice and my mother will have the champagne."

"Certainly," Helen doesn't crack a smile, but ushers in the models once Emily and Laura have their refreshments. The parade begins.

Out of twelve dresses modeled, Laura is only interested in trying on one. "I guess I should have done more homework." She whispers to Emily. The only one I have seen online I liked was Vera Wang and it wasn't very bridie."

Emily laughs uncomfortably and reaches for the petit fours they have brought out. "This is my breakfast," she lifts the petit four in her hand as if to toast Laura.

"Oh my gosh Mom, I wish you had told me."

"It's okay, champagne and cake for breakfast. I'm so urbane. This will do."

Laura loves hailing a cab in New York because there are so many of them and *it feels like they are hungry for passengers here.* They get in and rush to the next posh salon only to have a similar experience. Then it's on to lunch with Vincent at Katz's, his favorite place in Manhattan for corned beef sandwiches.

"Any luck?" he asks them as they pull out their chairs. "You got here in the nick of time. I had to bribe the waiter, and I thought I might have to roll up my sleeves and have a fist fight with that woman over there," he bows his head discreetly and shifts his eyes to identify a middle-aged woman, wearing a dress-length raincoat and sensible walking shoes. The kind that might have been purchased at Lands' End or Talbots.

Laura laughs, "Dad you are so funny, of all the restaurants in this city and you have to come to the biggest tourist attraction of them all."

"Sorry pumpkin, I have to get my corned beef fix."

Laura slumps into her chair and says, "No, dress yet."

"But we're having fun," Emily chirps.

Vincent surveys the room. "Yes, this is a great adventure, isn't it?"

"So, Dad, Sean is going to wear a kilt. How about you?" She says trying to get a rise out of him.

"I've packed my tuxedo that travels well to any occasion."

"We can't talk you into tails?"

"Really? Are you serious?"

The waiter approaches their table and Vincent holds up three fingers. "Bring us three corned beef sandwiches, a stout... and what would you ladies like to drink?

"Well, I had champagne and sugar for breakfast so just a cup of coffee for me."

"Laura?"

"Ah, I'll have the lemonade," she says closing the unnecessary menu, and focusing on her father.

"You were saying you would wear tails if that's what your daughter wanted."

Vincent clears his throat and lowers his chin, then focuses back to eye level staring straight at Laura.

"If that's what you want, dear. I'll go to as many of your weddings as it takes to make you happy."

"Oh my, I've hit a nerve." Laura hands the menu back to the waiter. "Let's just see how the afternoon goes. The castle is quite formal."

"So, what happened last night in the Park?"

"Oh, I haven't told Mother, we've been too busy shopping."

"And drinking champagne." Emily grins. It is apparent that she is still a little buzzed.

"I wanted to let Cloud have some off-leash time after all day on the plane. That doesn't start until 9. It was a well-lit area and there were still people roaming about, but we ran into a bunch of boys who had been drinking. The pack leader was visibly smashed and got obscene with me. Cloud was off fetching the ball, or they probably would never have approached me.

"Cloud came to my rescue and eventually knocked the kid down. I was terrified they might have a gun or knife, but we got away without too much difficulty. I thought it best to let a New Yorker handle the Park today."

"Oh, that's unfortunate, Laura." Her father tells her. "You need to be a little more street savvy here in New York."

"I had Cloud with me. He's not going to let anything bad happen to me," she says, remembering how vulnerable she felt when Cloud was at a distance from her.

"Actually, Sean just sent me an iWatch that has a 911 signal on it. I did punch it but didn't stick around to see if anyone showed up."

"They have plain-clothes cops in the park. It's usually safe." Vincent leans back in his seat saying this to no one in particular.

"Oh my God, that sandwich looks good" Their food has arrived. Vincent rubs his hands together and turns his plate for better advantage to tackle the loaded bread ready to topple from a heaping serving of the juicy meat.

Vera Nails It

"That's the one, that's the dress I saw online. I love it!"

"Yes, that's the Maria Theresa from our fall collection. It features nude and ivory tulle asymmetrically pleated over an A-line skirt," says the Vera Wang sales associate, Delores who looks to be in her late fifties. *A real old-timer in this business of pedaling bridal gowns.* Laura observes.

Delores strokes the arm of the young model and fondles the lace lovingly. "The gold Chantilly lace is hand placed, making it a remarkably personal gown."

"I love it. It's the one. If it looks good on me."

"Let's go ahead and have you try it on, and we'll take your measurements for the ideal fit," Delores says.

"I leave for Scotland day after tomorrow," Laura says now panicking that there might not be enough time to make this gown hers.

"What is the actual wedding date?"

"August 26th."

"I think we can make that happen with an express package."

When Laura comes out of the dressing room to model the Maria Theresa for her mother and Delores.

"Oh, Laura it is exquisite!" her mother gasps.

"Well, it looked better on the skinny girl, but I love it."

"Nonsense, it looks like it was made for you."

Delores approaches and touches the dress delicately here and there.

"Bueno, come here please and give us some advice. Can you make this work?"

A tiny woman with a seamstress' tape measure dangling around her neck enters and begins to make tucks, writing her findings down in a little book. She smiles and nods to Delores.

"Very nice," the seamstress beams timidly at Laura. Then she pulls out her phone and takes several photos front and back.

Despite the tight bodice, Laura is able to raise both arms up as directed. "This is great. Our work is done here. Sean will love it."

"Now all we have to do is find shoes and we can go back to the hotel and rest," Emily says letting the oxygen deflate from her lungs as if she has been carrying a big heavy, oversized ball all day.

"Tight fit? Or loose?" Delores asks. "Most brides like to starve themselves until the big day."

"Well, I just had a giant corned beef sandwich and I'm close to 40, so let's not make it too tight."

By the time they find the perfect shoes to go with the gown it is close to 6. They decide to call Vincent and tell him to meet them at Frenchette, a hastily chosen restaurant based on their cab driver's recommendation.

"I feel like we should get you home Mom, you've had a long day."

"I'll rest tomorrow," Emily waves her hand looking more delirious than she would have liked to let on.

On the Set

Laura fights her urge to touch her face. She's done TV interviews before, but not in New York, and not with Gayle King. They have finished with makeup and she is sitting in the chair where she will be interviewed. She has asked not to be rushed and the crew has held to their promise. It is comforting to have Cloud there nearby.

Aside from talking about her new book, Laura has been told to be ready for personal questions about her relationship with Sean and the show, of course. *A new sober first. God, I hope I don't make a fool out of myself! I should have never agreed to this interview now, before the wedding. I'm jittery enough as it is.*

She is wearing the long flowing skirt she and the stylist had agreed upon for the interview and the fabulous ankle boots she bought for the trip. Despite the heat of the studio lights, they have the AC cranked down so much Laura has goosebumps.

Gayle comes up and pets Cloud. "He's so beautiful and well-behaved." Gayle tells Laura.

I am, aren't I? Cloud licks his right front paw nonchalantly pretending he is bored by all the hubbub of the television set. There are people running around everywhere and the smells coming from the breakfast bar include bacon and sausage. *And bananas. I love bananas!*

"Oh, he has his moments."

"I hear he defended you in Central Park, night before last."

Laura tries not to scowl. "Where in the world did you hear that? Please, I don't want to talk about that in the interview."

Gayle gives her one of those warm signature smiles of hers. "Not to worry. Usually the Park is quite safe. That was an aberration."

The countdown starts, and Gayle takes her place. "So, we have with us here…"

Gayle's ease is by design infectious, and Laura soon relaxes. Sharing her characters with the world from *Two Moons of Merth* makes time dissolve. *It's interviews like this that will help propel the book into bestseller status.* She reminds herself.

Gayle goes straight from the book, gliding through a flawless transition, to asking her about the mystery of who her grandfather was. It is evident she is laying groundwork for a station break "tease," but Laura deflects the line of questioning.

"Gayle, I appreciate your interest, but it's a complicated personal issue for me and my family. If you haven't already seen the pilot as over five million viewers have, you should stream it." *I don't know where that came from, but thank you God, for that bit of wisdom at the right moment.*

Gayle backs off, not missing a beat. While the station break is running, Gayle puts out her hand to Cloud. *Finally, someone is giving me the attention I deserve.*

"Cloud would you like to sit over here by me?" Gayle asks him. Cloud stands and shakes. And then moves over in front of Gayle's Chair. "Well, I'll take that as a yes," she laughs. "He seems to be at ease here."

"That's my boy. Always happy to oblige. Give him a piece of sausage and he'll follow you anywhere."

Gayle smiles and turns toward the camera as soon as she is signaled. "Welcome back. And if you are just tuning in, we are visiting with author Laura Haskell and my new-found friend Cloud, one of the ghost-seeing dogs on the newly launched FilmFlix show, *Ghosts are Real*." She leans over slightly and gives Cloud a head stroke. "Ooh, his fur is so soft." They exchange more friendly banter about the wedding and "what is next for the couple."

When the interview is over Laura's adrenaline rush has left her as limp as a rain-starved tulip. She and Cloud make their way down to the street and the waiting car. The moist air on her face gives her a new resurgence of energy. "We're in the home stretch now," she tells Cloud. "All we have to do is get on the plane in the morning." *I have a gorgeous dress and the man I love. The rest will take care of itself.*

Cinderella

There was never a time Laura could remember feeling euphoric for such an extended period of time. Perhaps it was because of all the people gathered to bless her and Sean's union as a married couple. The castle grounds are stunning and the few days before the wedding are spent just enjoying the friends gathered. Activities like croquet on the lawn are made jovial by all the men who dress in kilts and ham it up.

Each night the film crew sets up movies featuring the resident ghosts and great drama is put into the telling of the history of the castle. Watching the sunset from the terrace while "Arnie" plays the bagpipes is a gathering no one wants to miss.

Meeting Michael and Harriet, Sean's grown children, for the first time is not as complicated as Laura has projected. Michael lives in Glasgow and has his own accounting business. Harriet has just graduated from Trinity College and is soon to start her first job as a fourth-grade teacher. Sean is working on both of them to come work for Wilson Enterprises, but he is hobbled by a long-established distrust of his 'close encounter' business as they straightforwardly call it, delivered with a bit of a sarcastic tone.

Sean privately pouts to Laura. "They've always been brain-washed by their mother."

"Give them time. There's a lot going on and they are attending their father's wedding to someone other than their mother. You've got to let things happen in their own time."

Laura catches herself. "I can't believe I just said that. That's your speech."

He grins and tells her she is right.

With all the people gathered Sean and Laura want to make the most of every minute, but they never seem to have a moment alone. The night before the wedding and after the lavish rehearsal dinner, they are lying in the century-old hand-carved bed, and are propped up by a half dozen luxury down pillows encased in fancy cutwork Irish linens. "I'm so tired," Laura says snuggling under Sean's arm. Cloud has been relegated to the foot of the bed, where he is already snoring softly.

"I just love everyone that works for you," Laura tells Sean.

"I do too, they are a special bunch," he says nodding off.

When Cloud begins to growl, they both look up "What is it boy got another ghost?" Sean asks him as he reaches for his laptop on the bedside table.

"Oh no, Sean, we need to rest. Please no ghost hunting tonight." The colorful ghosts who haunt the castle, at this point, are well documented. "Surely you've already filmed them all."

"You're right," he lays back down, his eyes half-closed as he hits the bed.

"Woof!" *Guys, you just have to see this guy.* Cloud is looking at a knight in armor carrying a bloody axe.

"Shush! Now go to sleep!" Laura warns.

Trauma Drama

"Sean... Sean where are you?" Laura reaches for Sean like she is surfacing from deep water, her arms thrashing for the surface, but he is not there next to her. She rolls over and the pain in her head, like an errant pinball, rolls around in her skull. *Oh my God, where am I?*

She looks around the room and realizes she is in a hospital bed. *But where?*

"Somebody please help me!" Both arms, and most of her fingers are attached to some kind of cord. Her body is prisoner to an entanglement of monitors. "Help me!" she shouts again. Her heart is racing toward sheer panic. Finally, a teenager in a nurse's uniform appears.

"Where am I?" Laura shouts, unable to suppress her anger.

"Please Ms. Wilson, try not to pull yourself loose from the monitors." The girl places her hands on Laura's forearms to prevent her from pulling loose from the monitors.

Wilson? Why did she call me that? Pain begins to thrust at her skull again.

"I'm sorry but what the hell is going on? Why am I here?" The petite nurse looks around the room furtively, not knowing exactly what is expected of her. She has been told to not say anything to Laura concerning her condition, and yet she doesn't want to look incompetent either.

"Dr Raun is in surgery this morning."

"And who the hell is Dr. Raun. And what's wrong with me?"

"You were in an auto accident. That's all I can tell you." The young girl is still emotionally numb from an argument with her boyfriend the night before. He had slammed the door and not returned. It was all she could think about. Would he call her today?

"I can't remember anything. What happened?"

"Memory loss is to be expected. Let me get the head nurse for you," the girl says as she races out of the room.

"Wait!" Laura calls, but the girl is gone. She slumps back down onto the pillow trying to prop it up a little as best she can with all the tethers she has to manage. Every time she moves her head clangs with excruciating pain. She winces involuntarily. Using her left hand, which is the least encumbered of the two, she fumbles around on her body and discovers a cast on her right leg. *At least both legs are there!* She tells herself.

A nurse, in her mid-forties wearing dark red scrubs comes into the room. "Mrs. Wilson, we are thrilled to see you awake. You've given us quite a scare several times," she says with a tone of gratitude delivered in a mild European accent.

Wilson, that was Sean's last name. She looks down at her hand and gasps. *Where is my exquisite blue diamond ring? I remember the afternoon he gave it to me.* The memory floods her psyche like ice water on a hot grill. *So much is not there.* Panic roils through her body like a slow jolt of recalcitrant electricity.

"Where's my ring?"

"Don't worry, all your valuables have been placed in the safe." The nurse flashes her a compassionate smile.

"Your mother asked us to call her the minute you awake. She was here, but she had to go back home. We honestly didn't know when, or if, you would regain consciousness.

"Can you get me my phone? I would like to talk to her."

"It's right there on the bedside table. We put it on a charger for you." The nurse moves to get the phone for her and assist her with it, despite the fact it's within Laura's reach.

"I don't remember her number," Numbness encapsulates Laura, robbing her of breath.

The nurse laughs. "Oh, don't worry I'm sure it's in your phone." She picks up the smartphone, presses a few buttons, and says, "Yes, here you have her listed as "Mom" just like the rest of us. Who can remember phone numbers anymore when we don't have to?"

"Would you like to Facetime so you two can see each other?"

"Sure," Laura responds although she is consumed by mental fog, and not confident about the question or the proper answer.

"Laura! You're awake. Thank God!"

"Mom? I'm a little sketchy. Having memory issues."

"Of course, that's to be expected."

"Where is Sean?"

"Oh honey," Emily turns her head away hiding the tears, but here is no disguising the trembling of her voice. It is clear to Laura that something is terribly wrong.

"I need to be there with you, but your father was having health issues himself, and we had the dog to take care of."

"Cloud? Where is he?"

"He's here, and his leg is healing fine." Emily flips the camera to view Cloud lying on the floor with a cast on his right rear leg.

"Oh my God, Cloud!" Laura shouts.

Cloud peers into the camera and whines. *I hear Laura's voice. She is alive!* He barks at her small image on the phone Emily is holding and Laura bursts into tears. Her body and her mind are fractured into tiny shards of pain. And it is all she can do to assemble a few snatches of her present reality.

"So, what's the matter with Dad?"

"Well, we stayed on a few days after the wedding so he could play some golf, until he had an incident. I left him in Scotland while I flew to Switzerland when you had your wreck. I wanted to stay there with you until you came out of your coma, but they didn't know when that might be. I needed to get your Dad home as soon as possible to his own doctors. So, I've been jumping back and forth across the Atlantic like a crazy woman."

"Mother is Sean gone?" Laura pleads through the spasms wracking her body.

"Miss Laura, you've had enough excitement for one day. You need to rest," the kindly nurse reaches for the phone and snatches it out of her hands before Laura can clamp down on it. "Yes, I will tell her," the nurse replies to Emily.

"And where in God's name am I?" She asks the nurse.

"Your accident was near Lake Lucerne. You and your husband were medevacked here to Geneva University Hospital."

"I want to see my husband." Laura demands.

The nurse takes a deep breath and tells her that Dr. Raun will be here soon to discuss all details of the accident. "Your mother asked me to tell you she is booking a flight as soon as she gets off the phone and hopes to be here tomorrow."

"Glad to see you have made it back. May I call you Laura?" Dr. Raun, with his long legs and dark curly hair, has entered her room. He wears heavily rimmed glasses which he looks over to talk with her. Laura can tell by the slant of the sun it is late afternoon. The doctor carries a tablet and refers to her chart with an upswipe of his fingers. He is wearing scrubs and exudes a physical strength that carries him through long hours on his feet as a surgeon.

"Where is my husband?"

"He is still unconscious."

She knew this and yet when the physician tells her, it is like a deep cut to her heart. The words surprise her as they calmly come out of her mouth.

"Is he going to be all right?"

The doctor looks at her carefully, focusing on her recovery and not of the other patient in another room who will not likely make it.

"Laura, we have been conservative in the way that we have been treating you. You may not know you are pregnant."

"What? You've got to be kidding."

"No, I'm not kidding. Is this a surprise to you?"

"Well, I had stopped taking hormones months ago, I didn't actually think anything would happen."

Raun gives her a funny smile. "You do know what causes pregnancy, right?"

She wrinkles her nose awkwardly; uncomfortable he is treating her like some sort of stupid teenager. "I mean, I'm close to forty, and my husband is 56." The fact that she has a baby growing inside of her doesn't register on her radar.

"What kind of drugs have you been treating me with? I'm in recovery."

"Well, it's good you are pregnant then, because of your condition we did not give you any hard drugs like morphine. We had no way of knowing you were in recovery."

"Where is my husband? Is he alive? I want to see him."

Dr. Raun smiles and takes a deep breath. "His prognosis is not good. Several of his ribs punctured his lungs. We operated immediately and we have done what we can for him, I'm sorry Ms. Wilson, but we don't expect him to last much longer. He also has extensive brain injuries."

"Oh…my God." Laura tries to breathe. It's as if all the air in the room as been sucked out and flushed down some hellish toilet. "Is he here in this hospital? Can I at least see him?"

Raun takes another deep breath contemplating the pros and cons of her request. On the one hand she shouldn't be leaving her bed for several more days. On the other hand, he could tell wild horses couldn't keep her from uprooting herself, and besides, seeing her loved one might work some magic.

"You are very weak and tied down to a lot of machines." He pauses and winks at her. "I tell you what, if you will cooperate with the nurses, I will authorize them to disconnect you from most of it for a short while. They can wheel you in to see him. He is unconscious. You can see him briefly. But that's it. That's all you're going to get. Then you need to come back here, eat your supper and sleep the rest of the night."

Contact

Fatigue swarms Laura as they disconnect everything but her IV and get her into a wheelchair. It takes two nurses to wheel her down the hall, one to push the chair and the other to wheel the IV stand. She is too weak to hold the awkward pole herself. At times she drops in and out of consciousness even though she is determined to stay alert, to connect with Sean somehow and bring him back to this world.

The room is dark except for a soft glow emanating from behind the closed drapes. *I thought it was still daytime.* All she can hear is the humming of some kind of machine and an occasional click from something else. Sean! *You are still here with me. How could this happen to us?* His hands are tucked inside the sheets like a baby being swaddled.

Without thinking to ask for permissions she struggles to pull the sheet loose so she can grasp his hand. The nurse complies to help her although she visibly hesitates, looking toward the other nurse who has wheeled the chair. There is an almost imperceptible nod between the two of them. *His hand is warm but lifeless.* She squeezes gently hoping to recognize his pulse or some other indication of life.

Sobs erupt softly, but uncontrollably. The nurses fidget.

"Ms. Wilson you must remain calm." The words are terse and frantic.

"I'm sorry, please let me stay a little longer." She squeezes his hand determinedly.

"Sean, please, Please! Come back to me!" The lack of response terrifies her. Then there is a little flicker and the line on the monitor goes straight.

"Get her out of here!" The nurse whispers. Laura's chair is turned, and she hears noises of people shuffling. She is slipping into unconsciousness and the last thing she notes is the rush of air on her face as she is whisked down the hall.

A Different Kind of Recovery

"Laura, thank God you are awake!" It is her mother's voice she hears coming from across the room.

"I've got to go. She just woke." The words are muffled as Emily crams her phone into her large black Gucci bag on the table.

"Mother, it's so good to see you." She says reaching for her mother. "I'm lost … I hope you can help me remember." *And there it is.* A stabbing jolt of grief rattles down her supine body. "He's gone, isn't he?"

Emily jerks back her own grief to bolster Laura "I'm so sorry dear." She reaches for Laura's hand, still armored with tape and needle. They stare at each other without words.

"We must focus on getting you well. Thank God you are here in Switzerland where the medicine is incredible."

I don't want to get better. I want to die and be with Sean. As she allows her thoughts to surface, she feels her breath dissipate. It is no use, her body perseveres, and she swallows, sucking in a gulp of air, almost choking on it.

"You've almost slept through the entire day. I was afraid you were slipping back into a coma, but they assured me you were not." Emily gropes for words, still trying to think of cheerful topics to lure her daughter back to life. "Cloud is fine. He's been quite a joy around the house. The vet is promising to take his cast off in a few more weeks."

The words provoke Laura's curiosity. "So, what happened?

Cautiously Emily asks her. "So, what is it that you remember. Let's start with that."

"Unfortunately, nothing," the words stick in her dry mouth.

"Well, you remember me, and Sean, and Cloud."

"Yes, I remember arriving in Scotland. I remember Sean there, and you and Dad and all the guests that started arriving. I don't remember the ceremony itself. I don't remember our honeymoon at all." *Mother is sad for me. I should try to cheer her up.*

"There are pictures on my phone…"

"Show me those. Maybe it will spur your memory."

Then it surfaces like a whale breaching the ocean's surface.

"My God, did they tell you?"

"Tell me what dear?"

"Did they tell you I am pregnant."

"Oh my God! No, they didn't tell me. Oh Laura, this is wonderful news."

Laura carefully constructs a little smile for the occasion. "It's the news you've always been waiting for. And now we know where she comes from, we know who your father is and my grandfather."

"It's a girl, they already know that?"

"No," she says reluctantly. "I made that part up. They say they are not giving me narcotics, but I'm still a little loopy in the head."

"Laura this is … this is the silver lining to your tragedy."

"I still can't believe he's gone." Her tongue is thick between her teeth as she tries to talk. She peers out at the sunlight filtering through the hospital window and decides to confide in her mother. "I never thought I would get pregnant. Sean was the one that wanted a child. I don't know why; he has grown children. I don't have a place in my heart for a child, except that she will be his. I'm not sure I have a nurturing bone in my body. I live like an old spinster in a haunted hotel for, God's sake."

Emily squeezes her hand, worried that what Laura says is true. "What's important now is that you get your strength back so we can get you home."

Laura remains in the hospital for 10 more days, doing whatever physical challenge they request from her, to convince the medical team she is sturdy enough to travel. Emily remains by her side and by the time she is ready for her discharge they have accumulated a skeleton of the lost memories by watching videos of the wedding and going through all the photos and videos on her phone several times. Her memories are now like a bulletin board stuffed with Postit™ notes. Laura remembers planning the driving trip to London, Paris, Venice and Switzerland, but the substance of the trip is still parsed and confusing.

One picture in particular brings back a strange memory. They had asked the hotel clerk to take their picture before they left Lucerne. It was in front of the little hotel they had stayed in. The car was packed, and they were just about to leave. Cloud was acting strangely. He began barking and whining and acting like he needed a pit stop. "Mother it was just before the accident. He sensed something. We took him over to the park across the street, but he didn't do anything, so we made him get into the car. We could have avoided the accident maybe if we had delayed our departure.

"Well honey, I don't think that's possible he could have predicted the car accident."

"I know it is improbable, but maybe there was something about Sean that wasn't right. Maybe he was having mini strokes or something?"

Emily works to control her facial expressions with all the veracity of her professional demeanor. "Laura, I can't see any good purpose in this line of thinking."

"Don't you see, if we had listened to Cloud, if we hadn't been in a rush to get on the road, maybe we wouldn't have crashed into that wall."

Emily pats her daughter's arm tenderly and quietly listens.

"So, you ready to check out in the morning?" Dr Raun asks her that evening on his rounds.

"Yes, we'll stay in a hotel for a few days before getting on the plane," Laura tells him.

"That's a good idea. Once you get home to San Francisco you will need to set up an appointment with a neurologist and an orthopedic surgeon to follow up on what we have done here. I promised I would look for referrals for you, or you may see whomever you like. The nurse will go over all of that with you in the morning,

"Oh, she'll be staying with us for a few weeks while she convalesces," Emily pipes up.

"No mother, I'll be heading home as soon as I can."

"But the dog won't have his cast off yet."

"We can discuss this later."

"It's not such a bad idea to remain with your mother for a few weeks. You'll be walking with crutches for another four weeks at least" Dr. Raun reminds her.

Just smile and let them think what they want. "We'll see. I live in a hotel with a whole bunch of people to take care of me."

"But honey, you can't travel like this and there's Cloud to think of."

Just watch me. I need to get home. Then with a rude burst, reality drowns her thoughts as she realizes she can't go home and drink. *I'm pregnant, trapped forever. I'm not worthy of the love Sean Wilson had to offer. But then, where is he? He left me and now I have this huge responsibility to raise his child. No one can help me now.* She falls asleep that night in the hospital bed choking back the sobs that escape from her core like hot gasses surfacing, scalding her, scarring her.

Crossing the Pond

The trip over the Atlantic to Virginia is exhausting. They had reserved the front two seats in First Class, so the bathroom was close, but now Laura truly wonders how she will ever make it the next three thousand miles to get home. It is only when they pull up to the house she grew up in and Cloud is there to meet her that she allows herself a little peace.

Vincent opens the front door and Cloud plows out to greet them. With their driver's assistance, she has already gotten into the wheelchair.

Oh wow, she's here. I'm so glad to see you! Cloud pants, his tail goes whopping back and forth and he dives in to lick her face. Even though her right leg is sticking out, he manages to get his front legs in her lap for some real hugs. *She's injured like me. Where is Sean? Something is terribly wrong. I tried to tell them not to get in the car, but they didn't listen. There is something else different about Laura, she smells different. I can't quite place it.*

"Oh, sweet baby, I missed you so!" She buries her head in his velvety fur. "I've been so worried about you."

Aah, I have her back, but wait, he is here too, only now he's just a ghost. She must be devastated.

Vincent, who isn't looking fully recovered himself, greets them at the door. He is wearing his house slippers and insists on taking the luggage from their Uber driver.

"Let me take a good look at you Laura," her father visually assesses the situation and the wheelchair. "Your mother's been worried sick. Thank God you and the baby are both all right."

Emily nods her head as if to say, 'not now Vince.' And when he doesn't get it, she has to say it out loud.

"Let's take everything a step at a time. There is much to sort out."

"Of course, dear. Welcome home ladies."

"Maybe you could have Jeremy help us," Emily asks him.

"Oh, I let that silly home-care nurse go a few days ago."

Emily scowls. "What have you been eating?"

"I have my sources," he says. His eyes twinkle as he shakes his phone at her.

Cloud backs down off Laura's lap, sits and tilts his head at her.

"He's not with me," she whispers, her voice cracking.

Au contraire! You can't see him, but I can!" Cloud barks three times in short succession,

A tingle ripples down her spine. "Is it possible he could be here with us?" She looks to her father and mother, who, while they have witnessed the revolutionary technology for themselves, can hardly wrap their minds around what she is proposing.

"Honey, you are grieving. And healing. Can you just relax? We'll have a hot meal, and all go to bed." Laura can hear the exhaustion in her mother's voice and decides to lay low on the whole topic for a minute.

"I'm in charge of dinner," Vince proclaims brandishing his phone. They both help Laura to the couch and get her situated.

"Come here big boy." She pats the couch and Cloud jumps up.

"Honey, he's not supposed to be jumping up and down on things until his leg heals."

"Oh, I didn't know." But now that he's on the couch anyway, she whispers in his ear. "Is he here?" Two short barks have come to mean that Nanu is present. Cloud gives her the same short three blasts he made earlier. Her arms ripple with goose bumps. *Perhaps he has been with me ever since the hospital I just didn't know it.*

Patience

"Whoever is out of patience is out of possession of their soul" – Francis Bacon

God, I want a drink! Laura's every living cell screams for escape from her reality. "I'm stuck here like I'm in prison," she tells Michelle over the phone. "The holdup is Cloud's leg. The airline will not allow him to ride in the plane with an injury. I will not consider putting him in cargo. I'm not doing that to him. That means I'm stuck here another week. That's what mother had to do to get him here, ship him in a crate."

"Honey, I feel for you. But I'm real concerned for that baby of yours. With you being in the place you're in… you is gonna' make a beeline for that airport bar."

"I'm terrified you're right."

"Did you get the videos of the weddin' I sent you?"

"Yes, thanks. I just wish I could remember it instead of watching it like it was some damn movie."

"Did they tell you the memories would come back?"

"Well, they certainly didn't promise anything. I've been making some progress, and I have a shrink I'm supposed to see once I get home. I didn't want to start that here for such a short time.

"Michelle?" she asks.

"Yes, honey."

"I need someone to help me travel home. I was going to fly my dog sitter out here to take care of Cloud on the trip, but maybe what I need is you."

"I'm listening."

"Well, why don't I send you a ticket. You will keep me away from the bars."

"Whoa, I can't keep you from drinking. You know, that right?"

"Michelle I can't stay here forever; I'm going bat shit crazy."

"Did you get to that meetin' we talked about?"

"Yes, I did. It was a huge ordeal. Dad drove me and helped me with the wheelchair and everything. I can't ask him to do that every day."

"He would do that for you. I met the man; he's great."

"He is, but he's supposed to be convalescing himself. I'm not going to ask him to take me again. Please! Come out here and come get me. I'll book your ticket and send it to you. Michelle, you know I hate to ask anybody for anything, but I really need your support."

There is an uncomfortable silence finally broken by a giggle. "I knew you was gonna' be high maintenance the minute I met you."

"Oh great! Thank God for you Michelle. Thank God."

"We gotta' get you back in the groove, sister."

"You know you've never explained that Southern accent of yours. You told me you grew up in Oakland."

"It's not Southern so much as black sass. My grandparents mostly raised me. They were from Arkansas, dirt poor farmers. Then they moved out West, when my momma crashed and burned, in order to take care of me. They thought they were going to save her from herself. That didn't work. They had a little BBQ joint in Oakland that became famous when the Giants discovered them. They often did catering gigs for some of the players. So, I grew up hangin' out with my grandparents and working at the Q-joint."

"I guess you did tell me about the restaurant."

"Wish they were still around, that was some good kinda' food." Michelle's voice trails off with her memories. "They tried to save me too. But I was too broken. Got raped at 15 and never looked back."

A sick feeling rises fast and furious in Laura to be reminded that this beautiful person had been so misused. Suddenly she realizes it is real puke scorching her esophagus. She reaches for the barf bucket she keeps nearby because it's too awkward to get out of the wheelchair fast enough when the morning sickness comes on.

"Oh Lord, I'm sorry you had to hear that. The puking has really started to kick in."

Michelle giggles, "Yeah this is going to be some kind of crazy trip."

He's Here in Our Midst

"Oh my, you've got to stop making me laugh," says Emily grabbing her stomach and wiping the tears from her eyes. Michelle has arrived and has been keeping them in stitches at the dinner table.

Mother seems to have completely relaxed ever since Michelle said she was coming to escort me home. She must be so worn out with all that worry and traveling on my behalf. Michelle keeps the humor coming and Emily is so giddy she nearly knocks over her wine glass. Vince is enjoying watching the three women giggle, encouraged there is laughter going on when so much has been lost.

Cloud whines and barks three times. "He's here you guys." Laura clutches at the arm of her wheelchair.

"Who would ever believe we are having dinner with Sean in our midst?" says Emily, but the humor has been sucked from the room.

"I've been thinking."

"Oh no, not again." Michelle says trying to restore the hilarity.

"I don't want anyone to whisper to a soul that he is here with me until after I get home and have my time alone with him. His computer is there, and I need to have some time for privacy before the FilmFlix people get into it with me. They will only be thinking of ratings." Laura's voice quivers and Michelle strokes her arm.

"Well, if you'll excuse me ladies, I'm off to bed," Vincent pushes his chair away from the table and Michelle and Emily start picking up the dishes.

"Yeah, our Uber will be here before you know it," Michelle says looking at her watch.

Flight from Hell

"I'm sorry Michelle, I didn't mean to be rude. My fake pain meds aren't doing much of anything and I'm anxious as hell to get home." Michelle is in the front seat, and Laura and Cloud, because of her cast, are in the backseat of a shiny new Jetta.

Michelle laughs. "I knew this trip was going to be hard, but for Christ's sake we haven't even gotten to the airport yet."

You can say that again, sister. You don't have to pee on fake grass that reeks so strong of strange dog's urine even I'm grossed out.

"I don't know how I'm going to keep from barfing," Laura says. I've brought all these bags in case, and all I've had to eat is crackers, but I'm so freaking nauseated.

"Here, let's roll down the windows," Michelle suggests turning around to emphasize her point. The Uber driver is looking uneasily in the rearview mirror. He was at first excited he had the famous dog as a passenger, but the thought of a pregnant woman getting sick in his car is more than he has bargained for.

Laura actually makes it to the airport bathroom before losing her crackers. She watches as the pink bile juice and soggy crumbs flush down the porcelain bowl. *I have really overstepped now. I'm exhausted and we haven't even boarded yet. And I'm cranky and sarcastic to Michelle. I will have to do better.*

Fortunately, they find a scooter car to carry them to the gate. Cloud rides shotgun, causing quite a stir. Not only is he a sight to see, but people are beginning to recognize him more and more as one of the 'seeing' dogs on the show.

Now this is the way to travel! Not as much fun as the Daimler, but Laura Boo is struggling to walk with those damn crutches. Frankly I'm a little worried.

The airline has done a good job of accommodating them. They are on the front row of first class, right next to the bathroom where Laura has room to stretch out her leg, still in a cast. A memory, like a stabbing pain in the gut hits her hard. It is of the afternoon when Sean proposed to her. *I can't live without him. Boy that's a bit dramatic Laura, suck it up. You have to accept he is gone. You are going to have his baby and you need to be a good mother.*

Laura has been told by her mother that at some point in the near future, she will regain her energy and she will stop puking all the time. *My God, she has been amazingly supportive. I should text her.* She looks over at Michelle across the aisle who is settling in with her seat mate. And begins to text.

...Mother you have been so patient and supportive. I couldn't have made it this far without you. I don't know how to make it up to you...

The bubbles come rippling back.

...Just take care of yourself and my grandchild and all is even...

...And that adorable dog...

...I'll come when it is time for the baby to be born...

Laura dozes off quickly and misses the first round of refreshments. When the flight attendant comes around with icy wash cloths, she accepts one gratefully. "I'm pregnant," she tells the attendant. It is the first time she has ever admitted it to a stranger. "Do you think I could have some juice and maybe some crackers? I'm getting a little weak."

"Sure ma'am. Is this Cloud, the famous ghost dog?" Hearing his name gives Cloud the excuse to whine. *I've been told not to bark, but I can at least make some noise.*

"I've been waiting to give him his treat. Is it okay?" The young man, prematurely gray and well-groomed looks like he might belong in a men's clothing commercial.

"Sure, of course." Cloud snaps at the morsel a little too aggressively for Laura, "Gentle." She admonishes him.

"We've got cranberry, apple and orange juice. Which would you prefer?" He asks her.

"Cranberry, and I'll take both the crackers and cookies you have brought. Don't judge me, I can't eat much of anything else."

But when the menus come out for first class, Laura can't resist ordering the tortellini plate because she is starving and close to the bathroom in case of emergency.

"You guys doing all right over there?" Michelle asks. The food, while it is just microwaved food, seems to be sitting well with Laura and she is beginning to feel at ease. She pulls out her book to read and is soon fast asleep. Until she is awakened by turbulence and everything, she just ate wants to come back up. The bathroom is occupied, and she is forced to pitch her cookies right there on the front seat of first class in a little bag supplied for this purpose.

Aach, that's nasty! So embarrassing. I don't understand why women want to have babies.

Michelle comes over to take the bag for her, and Cloud licks the tiny drop of her spittle that landed on her lap.

"Shit," she says under her breath. "I am so embarrassed."

Michelle pats her hand and whispers, "Don't be."

"Could you please get me some water?"

"Of course, honey. You just relax. It's okay. We'll be home in a couple more hours."

"Well, we're not landing until nine. Why don't you stay at the hotel tonight? I'll tell them to fix you up in a deluxe room," Laura pleads more with her sorrowful eyes than with her voice.

"I could do that, I suppose."

"Great! Sleep late and order yourself some of our blueberry pancakes from roomservice in the morning. Sean loved those." Tears burn hot and salty as they begin involuntarily to pool in her eyes.

Cloud impulsively jumps up in the seat he has been lying under for most of the trip and begins to lick her tears away. *Aww, don't cry Laura Boo. I'll take care of you.*

Then Laura is sobbing, she can't stop the tears and people begin to watch as the big white dog tries to comfort her. Next, she is both laughing and crying

"Oh my God, it's the hormones. Whatever you have heard about pregnancy it's true." She says, now laughing more than crying. "This is crazy. I'm an emotional wreck."

"It's okay, Laura," Michelle squeezes in on the chair with Cloud, which means she is mostly squatting with only one butt cheek planted.

Spotting someone in the row of chairs behind her seat filming the incident on their phone, Michelle scolds the woman and reports her to the crew.

"I'm sorry, you have to make that woman erase that video," she tells the flight attendant.

"I'll see what I can do." He reports back later and says the woman already sent it to a friend and the only thing he can do is put her on the "no fly list." A huge smile overtakes Michelle's sour mood.

"That will make me very happy."

"Can I have her contact info so I can sue her?" Laura asks, halfway believing she might.

"No, ma'am, you will have to get a lawyer involved to get that kind of information, but I will tell you she is sitting in seat 2F."

Laura chuckles, punching the flight number, date and seat number into her phone. She will never follow up, but the action makes her happy.

First Contact

Laura is completely wiped out when they get back to the Crescent. Despite her obsession to make contact with Sean, all she can manage is to crawl into bed.

She sleeps to nearly nine the next morning and jumps up to both pee and puke. *This is getting to be way too normal.* She stumbles around on her crutches until she finds his backpack in the closet. She crushes it to her chest and inhales his scent. The fog of her emotions leaves her breathless.

"Cloud, Come!" Her command is not necessary. He is already at her side.

She hobbles to the couch with the backpack and Cloud lowers his head, making it easier to put the head gear on. She stabs at the keyboard with a blundering voracity. The adrenaline pumps hard and fast rendering her fingers useless. *Slow down! I can do this.* The screen on the computer asks her to put in a password. *SHIT! What is it?* Memories from before the accident are more readily available to her than a week ago, but she is at a loss for what the password is. *I know I've used it.* Then with a sting of recognition she remembers. *Yes, of course it is <u>Cloud</u>! I remember the day he created his passcode. It was right after Mark the Magician had come. Prior to that Sean hadn't used a password, but the tech team insisted. They didn't want his laptop to get stolen and their work to get hacked.*

"God Sean, I miss you!" her head drops, and the sobbing starts again.

With the headset on Cloud becomes impatient. *Come on, Laura Boo, pull it together.* He circles and tangles the wire.

"NO! Be still Cloud." She focuses and types in his name. Unfortunately, the computer does not respond. Fear continues to bludgeon her capacity to think and she doesn't have control of her own fingers. *What the hell am I doing wrong? Think Laura, think.* Then a thought, like a feather sifting downward, settles in her mind. *It's all caps.* She types again and the password page drops from sight.

"I'm in!" she declares to Cloud. The computer is not in the ghostware, as Sean liked to call it, but in a word processing mode. She backs out of it, so obsessed by the idea of contact that she doesn't realize the treasure of his personal computer in her hands. She searches for the Casper-looking icon and clicks. A wave of chill bumps spreads across her forearms.

"Where is he?" she says out loud to Cloud who is whining and searching the room.

"There! There he is! Oh, my God, there he is!" Sean's image approaches the couch and sits down turned to face her. She reaches out to touch him and of course there is nothing reciprocated. This miraculous software, so revolutionizing, turns inadequate as he flashes one of his disarming smiles. The clarity of his image is more blurred than she remembers from previous experience. She knows on television the images are visually enhanced, but his image is *greatly disappointing.*

"Damn, Sean, I need you. Why did this have to happen?" The icy tingle of chills, like an Aurora Borealis, billow across her body. "I don't remember our honeymoon, for God's sake."

"Do you know I'm pregnant with your child? Please just respond with something!"

Then, much to her surprise, though she has requested a sign from him. His smile turns bittersweet and his face falls to something akin to grief.

"Don't be sad. I will raise her right. I will. I promise. You have changed my world. I am a better person because of you."

The doorbell rings and his image disappears.

Pancakes and Proverbs

Laura sucks in her breath, gathers her crutches, and goes to the door to greet Michelle.

"Did you get some rest last night?" Michelle asks her as she enters.

"I suppose."

"Well, let's have some of those pancakes you were bragging about."

"Oh, I haven't ordered anything to be sent up yet. I thought you were going to have breakfast in bed."

"Nope, I wanted to check in on you before I leave. I called the office and told them I wouldn't be in 'til lunch."

"Well, I'm actually hungry. Let me get something going."

"I saw Sean this morning," Laura says as she dials the kitchen.

"How was it?"

"Not completely satisfactory," she says before the kitchen answers. "This is Laura, please send up two blueberry pancake orders with the works for my guest and I." Laura turns to Michelle, her agony visible, kinetic, like lightning before rain.

"I had such high expectations."

"I know honey," Michelle consoles her with a slight touch on her arm. "Believe me, I know. On the trip you bit my head off if I even thought of something that didn't carry us straight home. As if the airplane would get us there any faster if I didn't take too long in the bathroom."

Laura winces. An embarrassed smile rises on her face and settles there. "I'm sure I behaved poorly. I was obsessed. What's ironic is that I crashed and burned last night. It wasn't until this morning that I got the equipment out."

"The Lord is close to the brokenhearted and saves those who are crushed in Spirit."

"What'd you say?"

"It's a Proverb, I was talking to myself."

"I've never known you to quote the Bible."

"It's the way I was brought up by my grandparents. I totally rebelled from that conservative upbringing and followed my mother into alcohol and drugs. Sometimes the Scripture just comes to me, like now."

Michelle pauses and looks directly at Laura. "I'd like to see him."

"Sure." Laura tries unsuccessfully to deflect her disappointment and fatigue.

"That is if you are up to it."

"Of course." She reaches for the laptop and Cloud lowers his head.

"He's compliant, isn't he?" Michelle says.

The soft whirr of the laptop emanates as she opens it and begins the process of starting the software.

When the picture is up, Sean is standing near the fireplace underneath the provocative portrait of Sally. He is wearing the Hawaiian shirt she bought him in Mexico. He smiles at her this time optimistically. "It feels like he sees us, but so strange to see him this way."

"It's freakin' weird!" says Michelle who has never witnessed the AI ghost experience.

Life!

A soft rainfall splatters outside on the stone veranda. Laura is sipping chamomile tea and Cloud is curled up at her feet in the window seat. The puking has ceased and desisted, and she has the smallest of baby bumps beginning to show. When drowsiness begins to wash over her, she lays down and curls up with Cloud for a rainy day nap. *Why not? Everyone has left me alone to mourn. I should take advantage of this time.*

As she dozes, she feels herself being nudged. *Mmm, Cloud must be readjusting his body. He's pushing on me.* "Laura, wake up. I want to talk to you."

"What? Oh, it's you Sean, you're here. I knew you didn't die."

"I miss you and I wanted to talk about our honeymoon. I heard you tell Cloud you don't remember it."

"Yes, that's right. Can you tell me now."

"It was incredible. We were having such a good time. I'm so sorry we crashed. The road was slick, and we spun out, crashing into that stone wall." His face twists gruesomely. "I'm so sorry you and Cloud were hurt. Cloud somehow knew, do you remember he tried to stop us from getting into the car that morning."

"Yes, you're right. We couldn't figure out was wrong with him. We were going to go up the mountain to hike. Oh, for God's sake why didn't we listen to him. I thought he was just being stubborn. I had no idea why he wouldn't get into the car."

"It was my time. You will understand some day." A crushing sadness engulfs Laura. *It's as if he is really here.*

"What was my favorite part? Tell me more about our honeymoon. I've been so sad not to remember it.

"Well, I was terrific in bed," Sean boasts.

"Of course, you were. You always are." She slips her hand between her thighs unconsciously.

"We had an incredible view of Paris, but we didn't go out much at first, well you know we were busy… so we didn't see much of the most romantic city in the world." He pauses to consider what she might have thought was the coolest part. "You really liked Versailles, you told me you'd never been there before. Or maybe it was our two nights on Lake Como, such a special place."

"I remember now, it was like being in another world"

"Well, sailing on Lake Lucerne was outstanding. I think maybe sailing is our thing."

"It is! Sailing is our thing we do together. You like to ski, but I'm not much of a skier, and well with the baby on the way." She pauses looking deeply at him for the first time since their conversation began. "You know I'm pregnant right?"

He beams at her; his image is crisp. She reaches up to feel the slight stubble on his face and reaches to kiss him. His lips are warm and moist. She can taste his breath. "I do, my love."

"I was furious at you when they told me you had died. But now you're, here aren't you?"

Cloud kicks her again reflexively in his sleep and she awakens to the sun now shining on the rain drenched stones of the veranda. It is only a dream, a dream like none other she has ever had. She rolls over and there it is a flutter deep inside of her. It must be life!

Getting Back into the Thick of It

The next few weeks Laura spends journaling all the memories about her honeymoon that flood into spaces in her brain that have been slammed shut and locked ever since the car wreck.

Then the phone starts ringing.

The first one to call is Stuart. "Just checking on you sweetheart. How is your health?"

"I'm off those crutches and my cast is off too."

"And the baby?"

"She's fine."

"She?"

"Yes, the doctor confirmed I'm having a girl, although I knew it all along." There is an uncomfortable pause in the conversation. "I'm still sober. If you're wondering."

"Oh, I had no doubt. You have the baby to think of now. Have you got a name yet?"

"No, I had thought maybe the female version of Sean spelling it Shawn, but my shrink thought maybe I should consider something else." The vision of Stuart on the other end of the line wearing a slick Gucci suit in the latest, most fashionable blue color, sitting behind his gargantuan desk tickled her.

"I'm not ready to do interviews yet, if that's why you're calling"

His pause indicates that's exactly why he's calling. She can hear him exhale a large breath.

"What about writing? Are you doing any of that?"

"No, but I'm journaling which is helping bring back my memories"

"Well, that's good. Are you getting out at all yet?"

"No, not yet, I can walk Cloud on a short walk. That's all I'm doing now. Still living the Miss Havisham existence."

"Well, I'm here to encourage you. I'm actually coming out to San Francisco next week. Maybe I'll stop by."

"Sure, that would be fun. Just let me know your plans."

The next phone call is much more traumatic. Marshall Crux, the young FilmFlix producer calls. She picks up the phone filled with dread in a way that makes her brain feel liquid. "Hi Marshall. What's taken you so long?"

"Laura we've been very concerned for you. I didn't want to intrude, but Stuart called and said you were on the mend,"

That's irony. I was once an obscure writer and now the whole world is knocking to exploit my life.

"I'd like to come see you soon. If that's all right?" *Here it is. I'll go ahead and address the white elephant in the conversation myself.*

"Yes, I've seen him. You know Cloud is a 'seeing' dog too. I'm going to keep the laptop. Sean gave it to me."

"Yes of course, no problem there. That is all owned by his company."

"What was it like?"

"Disappointing."

Marshall chooses to deflect. "Have you been in contact with Wilson Enterprises yet?"

"Melissa has checked on me several times. I don't know anything about the operation or what is going on."

"Don't worry about that, there's no one really in charge right now."

"His son, Michael, was at the wedding. I only met him briefly, but Sean had expressed an interest in getting him involved."

"That's right. I met him too."

"I have to face these things soon anyway. That company was more important than almost anything to Sean. I actually have Sean's phone. They gave it to me in the hospital." She looks down at her left hand at the blue diamond on her ring finger and the band filled with sparkling diamonds like stars all in a row.

"I'm only an hour away, in Los Gatos. Do you think I could come up and see you soon?"

"Sure."

"Is tomorrow too soon?" *There it was, the urgency.* Laura takes a deep abominable breath, reassuring herself she is supposed to see Catherine, her shrink, tomorrow at two.

"I have something at two, why don't you come up after that and stay the night here at the hotel. We can have dinner."

"Great, I'll see you around five."

Laura goes to the row of drawers in the closet that were to be Sean's. *If only he had had a chance to move in.* Mostly all that was there were a few things he had been wearing when he was visiting. There were eight or more hangers with some pants and some shirts, a bottle of his Armani cologne and a razor in the bathroom. That was about it.

She had taken out his phone and looked at it several times. It still worked. In fact, she had plugged it in to keep it charged, for a while, then turned it off. She couldn't stand the thought of answering it. This would be the day she would get it out and begin the business of 'calling up the past.' *Corny Laura.*

She decides to start by texting Michael. *A softer and easier way.*

...Michael this is Laura on your father's phone. Wanted to talk when you have the time...

It only takes minutes before the phone rings. She is still wondering if Michael is freaked out by his father's number coming up on his phone, but she was afraid if she used her phone, he might not recognize who was calling.

"Laura, I've been tryin' to call you. I've left several messages with the manager at the hotel."

"I know, I'm sorry. I should have called you sooner. And I'm sorry about the short notice on the cremation. A decision had to be made and I was still delirious. My mother did the best she could under the circumstances."

"We understand. Are you all right?"

"No, but I will be. Physically I'm coming around."

"I need to talk to you about your father's company."

"I know."

"We need to figure some things out. It was his wish that you join him in operating the company."

"Yes, we discussed it last summer. At that time, I told him to count me out. I have my own accounting firm in Glasgow, you know."

"Do you still feel the same way?"

"I'm not sure."

"You know he's here with me, his apparition."

Michael laughs nervously, "No offense, but that sounds so incredibly stupid."

"You were with him for several weeks; didn't you see what was going on?"

"Yes, but the whole thing kind of gives me the creeps. I don't share his passion for this stuff."

"There's something else I need to tell you, and you may not be keen on this idea, but I'm pregnant with Sean's baby."

"Well, that's nice for you." Michael says with as much grace as he can muster.

"Look, if you don't want to be a part of his company that's fine. It's quite a successful venture, and they are looking to me to give them some leadership. I wanted to give you the first crack at participating."

"I don't know what I could offer."

"Well, your business acumen for starters. The rest of it pretty much runs itself. FilmFlix is heavily invested as far as seeing the success of the company continue. I shouldn't have a difficult time filling whatever role I need even though it will probably take about four people to fill Sean's shoes."

"I appreciate the offer Laura. Let me think on it. Thanks for callin.'"

Moving On

The visit with Marshall turns out not so different than what Laura expects. Before dinner is halfway over, he has somehow talked her into one last episode where she reunites with Sean. "This is just so personal. I just don't think I can share it with the whole world." She explains to the young producer, halfway knowing as she states her desires, that she will cave because she owes it to Sean. This would be what he wants.

"On the one hand I feel like I am exploiting myself, and on the other hand if I don't do this, it would be devastating to Sean…Sean's memory." Stumbling over talking about him in third person is actually weird because she is in constant dialogue with Sean knowing that his apparition is always with her. And she uses the software daily, mostly in the evening to talk to him. His ghost is a most dedicated listener. There has been no further 'vivid' contact with him like she had in that one dream, *if that is what it was.*

"I want Chad Owens to narrate the program, and I don't want to be directly interviewed. You have to be cognizant you are dealing with a grieving widow."

"I understand. I think we can work with that." And in a gesture that is too mature for his age, Marshall takes her hand in his in a comforting way and looks directly into her eyes to reassure her. "We will respect your wishes."

Through the next few weeks, they correspond concerning the details and come up with a plan for a reduced crew.

"I'm so glad you came down a little early so that we could prepare and rehearse our presentation," she tells Chad when he arrives about a week later.

"I'm so terribly sorry this has happened, Laura. Sean was a unique individual who did so much for our industry, and for everyone really. There's just no way to replace him. He is sorely missed.

"I know the two of you were so in love. It was just obvious."

"Well, thank you Chad. This is confidential, but I don't mind telling you. I pick up that computer every day and talk to his apparition,"

Chad chuckles, "Well I don't blame you. I would too if I were in your shoes."

"Cloud enjoys the interaction too."

"Funny thing is my grandparents no longer seem to be hanging around. We still have other ghosts here in the hotel, but they have vanished."

"Really?" Chad leans over in the chair in which he has been sitting in Laura's living room and ponders this. The provocative portrait of her grandmother above the fireplace is nearby. "Many, many people talk about how a ghost remains here because they have unfinished business. It's folklore really, no science to it. From what Sean was talking about he seemed to lean toward alternate realities that might have to do with quantum physics."

Chad pauses and looks directly at Laura. "We may never know, but the fact that your grandmother identified your grandfather to you and your mother, well maybe that's all she needed in order to move on."

"That certainly seems plausible. I kind of miss her. If that doesn't sound strange. In fact, mostly because I know he is there, I feel Sean's presence throughout the day."

"Well, this pretty fellow," he says poking at Cloud, "he knows he's here and he probably signals to you a lot about where Sean's ghost is."

"He does, actually."

Epilogue

"Lizzie! Don't run off so far. You need to come back this way."

Cloud gives Laura a concerned look and bolts for the rambling four-year-old. The wind tickles his ears and he playfully nuzzles the golden-haired child, herding her to turn and race toward her mother.

They have come to look at some property that overlooks the Pacific just north of the city. There is a path down to the ocean where they will be able to take long walks.

Laura has decided that a hotel is no place to raise a child. *And I heartily agree. The sound of the waves will be with us every day. We can run on the beach and frolic in the surf. I can get away from all those creepy ghosts. Except for Sean, who is right here now. He will always be part of our pack.*

With Lizzie rounded up, Cloud jumps up on Laura something she has allowed him to do more now than in the past. *This is Heaven! We've got to do this.* He emphasizes his gesture by sneaking in a lick across her lower face.

"Yes, Cloud I know. This is wonderful. We are going to build a house with windows everywhere. Now please get down."

Author's Note

Dear readers, without you I am not an author. The tree may fall in the forest, but if no one hears it, then it doesn't make much impact. *Beyond* is my second novel, which makes me relatively new to writing fiction. That means I need ratings and reviews more than, say, Stephen King does. So, if you would be a dear and write reviews and post ratings on Goodreads, Amazon and the like... Woohoo!, it would mean the world to me.

CPSIA information can be obtained
at www.ICGtesting.com
Printed in the USA
LVHW031324241220
675070LV00007B/343